HONEY BEAR COSY MYSTERIES
HONEY MEAD MURDER

DAHLIA DONOVAN

HOT TREE PUBLISHING

ALSO BY DAHLIA DONOVAN

MARINE | THE BOTANIST |THE UNEXPECTED SANTA
|THE LION TAMER | HAKA EVER AFTER | COMPLETE
BOX SET

HONEY MEAD MURDER

HONEY BEAR COSY MYSTERIES
BOOK 1

DAHLIA DONOVAN

TANGLED TREE PUBLISHING

For information, contact the publisher, Tangled Tree Publishing.

www.Tangledtreepublishing.com

Editing: Hot Tree Editing

Cover Designer: BooksSmith Design

E-book ISBN: 978-1-922679-85-7

Paperback ISBN: 978-1-922679-86-4

To Meg, for sending me the initial video that inspired this series

ONE

MURPHY

"Oi. Mr Grump? Your carthorse has arrived."

Murphy stood up from where he was crouched down to inspect the latest delivery. "Carthorse? Hardly. I've already brought the delivery inside. And for the millionth time, Tea. I am not a grump."

"No, you just hate mornings, afternoons, people, sunlight, basically everyone but your lovely George." Teagen was, as always, immune to his glowering at them. "Well?"

"Hate is a strong word. I don't hate you." Murphy wasn't entirely sure he liked his best friend every day, but he didn't hate them. "Come on then, Tea. We've got a fresh batch of honey delivered yesterday. We also need to check on the two-year

1

casks. Probably want another year on them just to get them where we want the flavour."

For six years, Murphy had run Honey Bear Brewery. It had been a play on his nickname of Paddington, earned during his brief stint in the military, owing to his surname of Baird and his tall, stocky build. His dark brown hair and scruffy beard certainly didn't help put people off the comparison.

His grumbly stubbornness came from both his Irish and Scottish sides. His ma had always claimed he bore more than a passing resemblance to his great-granddad Murphy. She'd been so proud when he'd decided to continue the family tradition of running a brewery.

For the first two years, Murphy had gone with simple ales. But then, he'd developed a close friendship with a local beekeeper, George Sheth. The younger man had been struggling to sell his honey.

His pride and joy.

Inspired by George, Murphy had decided to begin experimenting with family recipes. Something from his Scottish side. His da had a collection of mead ones that dated back a century or more. It had taken some trial and error to get everything right, but his brewery and the small pub attached to it were doing well six years later.

"Well? Did you finally ask our playwright out?"

"Tea." Murphy shook his head at their teasing grin. "It's George Bernard Sheth. Not Shaw. Plus his ma's Scottish, not Irish, and his dad's from India, so I highly doubt either of them are related to a famed Irish playwright."

"Must you take all the joy out of my play on names and words? Besides if they didn't want anyone to make the connection, why name him George Bernard? Fine, fine. Well? Did you ask him out?"

"He's named for his ma, Georgie, and I think a great-uncle. And no, I... couldn't ask him out." Murphy leaned back against the table behind him. He dragged his hand across his face, pausing to scratch his beard. His blue eyes met their dark brown ones. He finally noticed they'd changed up their hair colour. "I like the green."

"Yeah?" They reached up to run their fingers along the shaved part of their head, tracing the line of the tight box cut. "I wanted a change. A little shorter trim. And the green fits."

"It does. What did your auntie say?" Murphy had known her for most of his life. When he was a young lad, she'd moved from Jamaica to Dufftown, a few houses down from his family. She'd taken in her brother's child when things had gotten difficult at home for them. "I sense her work here."

"Yep, she did the dye for me." Teagan was a bright soul. They were in their twenties—about ten years his junior. They'd bonded over their love of beer, history, music, and video games and become great friends. "Why didn't you ask him out? You're both so stubbornly blind to how much you like each other. You're perfect together. You both hate people."

"I couldn't get the words out," Murphy grumbled. "And I don't hate people. George doesn't, either. He just finds people confusing. And he likes his bees."

"Try miming or text messaging. Hell, how about I get you a homing pigeon?"

"I'm going to ignore you now, especially considering you haven't asked your crush out either." Murphy turned his attention back to the boxes in front of him. "Think we're ready for this new mead experiment."

Teagan gave him an excited grin. They enjoyed experimenting with flavours. "You know, we could be twins."

"Sure. Sure. Except I'm tall, white, and thirty-eight. You're not tall, black, and twenty-six."

Murphy hefted up the crate of honey George had dropped off for him earlier. "Though you're smarter and more charming than me or anyone I'm related to. Be grateful we're chosen family and not blood-related. You'd be far less magnificent as a Baird."

"Aw. You do love me. Should I note in my journal you've had your one feeling of the week?" Teagan teased him, laughing when he glowered at them. "And I'm telling your da you said he was daft."

"How about you give me a hand instead?"

Teagan came over to inspect the jars in the box. "What's all this then?"

"Early season honey." Murphy lifted out the jars to place them on one of the stainless steel tables in their workspace. "He's brought some from his first extraction, then probably in September he'll bring the last. So I thought we could experiment with the various depths of flavour each brings out in the mead."

"Small batch first? Make sure it's not utter shite before we waste an entire delivery of honey." Teagan grabbed one of the jars and then replaced the others into the crate. "Is George coming by to give us a hand with figuring out what to pair with his golden nectar?"

"Must you make it sound so salacious?" Murphy groaned.

"Do you want some of his golden nectar?" Teagan darted out of reach when he went to fling a wooden spoon in their direction. "Going to give him a text now. See if he wants to pop around to help us out."

"Tea." Murphy subsided when they'd already danced out the door. "Sodding nosy twit."

"I heard that, Paddington."

Ignoring them, Murphy hefted the crate of honey to the other side of the room to one of the tables set up against the wall. It was a little brewery attached to an existing pub on the edge of the small village. They'd made the most of the space.

It was perfect for two or three people. They had enough space for the casks of mead and for brewing. He kept the business small on purpose.

His da tried to encourage him to expand. A few pubs in nearby villages often asked him to deliver to them, but he was content. The brewery was a passion project for him; he wanted nothing more than to have enough to live comfortably.

Nothing more, nothing less.

He'd never been overly ambitious. There hadn't

been grand dreams in his childhood. All he wanted was to be comfortable and satisfied.

And to take pride in what he did. The brewery and pub were a success in his eyes, since they paid for themselves. What else could he possibly need in life?

"Paddington?"

"Hmm?"

"George is on his way over. He has a few suggestions for flavour pairings to go with the honey. Something about early in the season making it lighter and more delicate." Teagan stepped back inside. They hunted at the desk in the opposite corner of the room for the brewery journal. "We're a few days behind in our notes. We haven't even started the page for June."

"Can you manage? I want to run to the pub and check on Maisie and Graeme. They're setting up for the tasting party we're throwing tomorrow." Murphy braced himself for dealing with his younger brother and sister-in-law. He loved them both, but they were often a little much first thing in the morning. "On second thought—"

"You do not pay me enough to deal with them this early." Teagan immediately cut him off. "Does Maisie have a theme for this event?"

"Maybe we are twins." Murphy smiled at them. "Perhaps I'll give us both hazard pay this year. And Maisie has a theme of sorts. Something about 'in the mists of time'? I stopped paying attention. She mentioned dry ice."

"Graeme's not that bad."

"Then you deal with him."

"Coward." Teagan had already dug into one of the desk drawers to find a pen and a ruler. "Off you pop. I've got a journal to update."

"I should've stayed in bed this morning."

"And miss George?"

Murphy paused to consider. He'd put himself through far more than his brother if it meant spending time with George. "You're not wrong, but I don't have to like it."

"Grumpy bastard."

TWO

GEORGE

"Bumble? You awake in there?" George crouched down to where his beloved rescue pug had vanished underneath the table. He was in one of his many beds in the little cottage. "Come on. The day awaits us."

A snore was his only response. Bumble was his third rescue pug. He worked with a charity that specifically took in older dogs who often had health issues.

If George hadn't been obsessed with his bees, he thought he might happily have dedicated his entire life to rescuing pugs. The poor creatures. He hated how often people weren't prepared to care for their particular needs.

"Well?" George reached under the table to grasp

the edge of the blanket and slid Bumble across the floor to him. He chuckled when the pug licked at one of the many bees tattooed on his fingers. "Good morning to you too. Shall we get going? Don't you want to see Paddy and Tea?"

Shoving down the little bubble of joy thinking about Murphy always brought him, George lifted Bumble up into his arms. He sighed at the fur now covering his black T-shirt. His life was doomed to forever wearing a dusting of pug.

He carried Bumble into the bathroom and grabbed one of the cloths on a shelf across from the sink. The elder pug put up with his careful grooming with many a sigh and grunt. It was important to take great care with his skin to prevent health issues.

George set Bumble down on the floor. He grabbed a nearby brush and dragged it through his black hair. It was just past his shoulders, probably more than due for a cut. He made sure to moisturise his face and trim his goatee a little. "Well? Are we ready to see Paddy?"

Bumble wiggled a little and snuffled up at him. Murphy and Teagan were both favourites of his pug. They were also some of the rare people that George didn't mind spending his day around.

His cousin often teased him about being a

hermit. He wasn't. There was just a massive limit to his ability to deal with people.

Part of it came from finding noise, people, and many other things overwhelming. It wasn't until he'd been in his midtwenties that George discovered the reason for what his family often referred to as his "quirks." He'd eventually been diagnosed as autistic, late in life, partly owing to a biased belief that autistics tended to be young white men. The world was slowly changing. But it had been a struggle to get the diagnosis even after years of research had made him almost more informed on the issue than the first doctor he'd seen.

It had been a relief to have a name for all the questions that plagued him. He wasn't sick or dying of some mysterious illness. In fact, he was perfectly normal for an autistic.

With actual answers in hand, George's confidence had grown. He'd decided to move from his family home in Edinburgh to Dufftown, where his cousin Margo lived. A cottage had become available, and thus had begun his obsession with creating the perfect wild garden to encourage bees.

The garden had turned into an obsession with hives and bees. His friendship with Murphy had led to him experimenting further with types of flowers in his garden to see how they affected the yield and flavour. It had become a labour of love for him.

And allowed him to spend increasing amounts of time with Murphy.

Murphy.

Murphy had begun to be a problem for George. His crush on the man had only increased over the years. At this point, it was almost painfully embarrassing that he could never gather the courage to ask him out.

Ready and dressed for the day, George decided to do the mature adult thing. He'd put the problem off for another time. Bumble bumped into the back of his leg in an attempt to herd him towards the bedroom door.

"Are we hungry?" George chuckled when Bumble headbutted his leg a second time. "I'll take that as a yes. No need for violence this early in the morning."

With Bumble ambling along beside him, George made his way into the kitchen. He grabbed one of the dog food packets out of the fridge and emptied it into a clean bowl. There was much snuffling and grunting from below when he took time to flick on the coffee maker before placing the dish on the floor.

"Here's your brekkie. I'm going to have a quick

check on my darlings." George left Bumble to his breakfast and went out the backdoor into the garden. He paused to run a hand gently over some of the phacelias growing close to the cottage. "Hello, lovelies."

A winding path led through his wild, secret garden. When George had moved into the cottage, he'd immediately set up a somewhat chaotic masterpiece with the sole purpose of providing for his bees. He kept most of the lawn un-mowed during summer and only did it once a month for the rest of the year.

It was wild and beautiful. Everything smelled lovely so early in the morning. The calming hum of insects was periodically disturbed by birdsong or an errant car horn in the distance.

There were times when his garden reminded him of his mind. Calm and chaotic. Wild and organised. A perfect dichotomy that confused those who didn't care to understand the purpose.

The cottage itself was nondescript. A small, old stone structure. It was charming in a fairy-tale way, especially with vines trailing up the outer walls.

It had been renovated ten years earlier by the previous owner, and George was grateful. The more modern appliances and the open floor plan suited his needs perfectly. He didn't need more than a single bedroom, ensuite, and a small kitchen and living room.

He lived alone with a dog. What more did he need? The garden had been what drew him to the property, after all.

It was larger than most in the area, and much of the garden had been untouched. So George had quickly gotten to work creating his perfect outdoor space. The only structure he'd added aside from beehives was a little shed for a workshop to keep his tools safe, dry, and out of the cottage.

After a quick inspection of the various sections of the garden, George continued down the path to where it opened out into a field with several rows of beehives. He preferred the British National style for the ease of maintenance and how efficient they tended to be.

Everything looked fine from a distance. Unfortunately, George didn't have the time to do a closer inspection, since Murphy was expecting him to pop by the brewery. It would take far too much time to don his beekeeping garb and thoroughly check each of his hives.

"I'll be back, darlings." George spent a fair amount of time in the garden or with his bees. There was always something to do.

To some, his family included, it likely seemed as if he preferred the company of bees, flowers, and his dog to humans. They weren't wrong. But he had a select few people who didn't aggravate him.

A very small, select few.

Returning to the cottage, George found Bumble snoozing contentedly on the rug in front of the range. His bowl had been licked completely clean. The coffee maker gave a beep, interrupting him when he went to take yet another photo of his pug.

His phone had nothing but images of either Bumble, the bees, or flowers. The latter two he often sent to his online group of beekeeper friends across Scotland that shared advice on maintaining the hives, particularly during the difficult winter months. They'd been crucial to his success.

Summer was really his favourite time of year. Everything came alive, and he had honey to harvest. It often felt like he was living in a magical fantasy world.

While bees had been his obsession since childhood, George's practical knowledge had been severely lacking until he'd moved into the cottage. His parents had allowed him to help a neighbour with their hive but he had never had one of his own. However, he'd more than made up for the lack now.

His friends in the online forum had filled in all the gaps in his knowledge. They were a great resource. He'd felt so much less alone in his love of bees when he'd realised they were all equally keen.

"Don't get too comfortable, Bumble. We're going to be off to see Murphy and Teagan soon." George quickly sorted his own breakfast: toast with his own honey and a strong cup of coffee. He stood by the sink, staring out into the garden and munching on his breakfast. "What do you think, Bumble? Think it might rain later. Clouds are gathering up nicely."

Bumble grunted in his sleep. George decided to take that as a yes. He swallowed his last bite of toast and chugged the last of his coffee before rinsing his sticky fingers in the sink.

"How do we look?" George hefted Bumble up to inspect them in the large mirror near the front door. "Painfully normal."

It took a few minutes to get his old Range Rover running. It was ancient. He'd bought it off a local farmer for a pittance.

The thing ran most of the time except when the weather turned frigid, then George had to coax her into running. That mostly involved cursing and talking nicely to the vehicle while Bumble stared at him like he'd lost his mind. He breathed a sigh of relief when the engine started up right away.

"Ready?" George secured Bumble in his little car seat in the back. "Let's go see our friends."

The drive into Dufftown didn't take long. George pulled onto the narrow lane that led to the brewery. Bumble perked up immediately; he tended to recognise when they were getting close to Honey Bear.

Teagan and Murphy stepped out to meet them. Bumble immediately went over to them once George had set him on the ground. He tried to stay cool and collected while noticing how the jeans and flannel shirt fit his crush a little too well.

George stared blankly for a few seconds before managing to blurt out a greeting. "Hello."

"Hello." Murphy had been just as slow, so George didn't feel quite so bad.

"Oh, my days. Is this why you haven't asked each other out yet? This is so fucking painful." Teagan had crouched down to pick Bumble up in their arms. They muttered to him about the fools around them. "More than painful. Honestly. Can I please move things along for you?"

"Tea." Murphy groaned from behind the hand now covering his face. "Not helping."

"Consider me your faery godperson." Teagan grinned a little maniacally at them. "Someone has to help. This is pitiful."

"*Teagan.*"

They completely ignored Murphy and continued speaking. "Bumble? When two men care about each other very much, they sometimes decide to date. To go on those outings, they have to actually ask each other. How have you never even managed it up to this point?"

"Teagan." Murphy sounded increasingly desperate to stop them from speaking. "We'll figure it out."

Smothering down his urge to laugh hysterically, George resisted the desire to flee. It was thrilling to know Murphy apparently felt the same way about him. But it was also mortifying to have another person have to throw it in their faces.

"It's been years. Are you going to be hobbling along on with a cane when you finally muster up the courage to ask him out for dinner?" Teagan heaved a massively dramatic sigh. They glanced between the two of them, then down at Bumble in their arms. "Why don't we see if we can find you a snack?"

THREE

MURPHY

THE AWKWARD SILENCE ONLY INTENSIFIED WHEN the door banged shut behind Teagan. George was inspecting a random scratch on the hood of his Range Rover. He appeared intent on pretending Murphy didn't exist.

Murphy had fully intended to ask George out on a date eventually. He had. Honestly, now he feared Teagan's intervention would spoil his plans. The ones that had existed before his best friend opened their big mouth to help. "Sorry about them."

"They're not wrong." George's gaze darted up to his before returning to his inspection. "At least, not on my behalf. I've wanted to invite you to the cottage for dinner a thousand times, but the words keep getting stuck between my brain and mouth."

Murphy found most of the tension dissipating in an instant. It was easier to contemplate asking him out when the answer was a foregone conclusion. "Would you like to be my date at the mead tasting event tomorrow night? Small crowd, so you shouldn't feel overwhelmed. You can wear your noise-cancelling headphones. Maybe we can grab something to eat when it's over?"

"I would."

Murphy couldn't stop grinning like a fool. He snickered in amusement with George a second later. "Tea's right. We're hopeless."

"Well, at least we can be hopeless together now. For a date. I mean, it's just a date." George groaned loudly before laughing for a second time. "We are pathetic at this."

Murphy thought perhaps it mattered more to them because of the developing feelings between them. "Maybe we shouldn't tell Teagan. They'll only laugh at us."

"Good plan." George went to grab the small box of honey from the back of his vehicle. "I've brought some of the late-season honey from last year. It's darker and richer in flavour. Not as delicate. I think we can compare and contrast the early season yield from this month."

"Brilliant idea."

"Since I swapped out a lot of the flowers in my garden last autumn, I'm guessing we'll see a slight difference in flavour as well." George waxed on enthusiastically about the native bushes and plants. They were all flourishing for him. "Sorry."

"Don't be." Murphy enjoyed listening to him. George had an almost melodic tone to his voice that he'd always found soothing. "You being so chuffed only makes me even more excited to begin playing with the next iteration of mead."

"I've had some ideas for your mead. I've done some research online. Early season honey might make for nice summer meads." George shifted the box under his arm. His dark brown eyes were bright and full of excitement. "You've talked about wanting to try a berry series. How about pairing the lighter honey with either strawberries and mint or perhaps blackberries? My late September yield should be darker and heavier. It would be brilliant with orange and maybe some sort of spices."

On the top of his list for the year, Murphy had wanted to play with a fruit or berry series of meads. A small batch just for the summer. Teagan had helped him sort through ideas a few weeks prior. He couldn't help grabbing onto the idea from George.

"Perfect. We've already started on recipes, so your ideas will fit right in." Murphy took a risk. He threw his arm around George's shoulder and dragged him closer. "I'm glad you're here."

"I've only come through the village, not across the ocean." George leaned into him for the briefest second before pulling away when they heard a shout behind them. "I'll... just go inside to check on Teagan."

With a groan, Murphy turned to find his brother and sister-in-law heading towards them. He chuckled when the brewery door opened and shut quickly. Unfortunately, George didn't have the fortitude to deal with the extroverted couple.

"Oi. Thought you were popping in to check on the preparations?" Graeme dragged him into a hug like they hadn't seen each other in years. "Honestly. Are you avoiding us on purpose?"

"Graeme." Murphy winced at the volume of his brother's voice. He always seemed amped up a few degrees more than everyone else around him. "I'm sure everything's fine. I've got work to do this morning."

"Ohhh, work. Work, he says. The big man has work to do this morning." Graeme teased in him a singsong tone. "What do we think, Maisie?"

"Definitely work. Important stuff." Maisie winked at Murphy, grabbing her husband by the arm. "C'mon, Graeme, we haven't finished in the pub."

"Is George here?"

"Graeme. Maisie." Murphy turned serious in an instant. He knew they were harmless and cheerful souls, but he wouldn't have them bothering George. "He's helping us with a new set of recipes. Leave him be. You hear me?"

Graeme placed his hand on his heart, giving an overdramatic sigh. "I'm hurt. Appalled that you'd think I'd bother the poor lad. All I hope to do is bring you two sweet lovebirds together so you stop pining from a distance."

"I see him at least a couple of times a week. So how is that pining from a distance?" Murphy rolled his eyes at the dramatics.

"Distance isn't always physical, Paddington." Graeme snickered at him. He held a hand up when Murphy glowered at him. "Pax. Listen, we came out for a reason."

"To annoy me?"

"We've got a couple coming today to check out the pub because they want to host an event. They'll be at the tasting tomorrow as well. Thought the owner might meet with them?"

In all honesty, Murphy thought the worst part of running a brewery with a pub attached to it was having to meet with people. Play nicely. Be polite. Customer service. It didn't come naturally to him, which had been the main reason he'd brought his Graeme and Maisie into the business in the first place.

"Fine," Murphy grumbled. "When?"

"They should be here soon. Ronald and Ella Donelson." Maisie glanced quickly over at Graeme. "I...."

Murphy briefly considered disappearing into the brewery and locking the door. "What's wrong with them?"

"You'll see. Not sure I have the words or ability to adequately explain Ronald and Ella Donelson." Graeme pointed behind him. "Here they come now."

Ronald and Ella Donelson turned out to be a middle-class couple in their forties who desperately wanted *everyone* to know how *unbothered* they were by their own money. They dressed a little too fancy for a small village pub. Their clothes were a bit too pressed.

"One does enjoy supporting the local business

on occasion." Ella brought her hand up to Murphy, who raised an eyebrow at Graeme, who was trying desperately not to laugh. "But one prefers to see the establishment before recommending it."

"Right." Murphy shook her hand firmly, refusing to kiss it like some knob in a movie. "Why don't we show you the pub? We'll have a few meads to test tomorrow...."

Ella grimaced while removing her hand from his. She plucked a handkerchief out of her purse and wiped her fingers off. Her husband opened his mouth, but she spoke over him. "Never mind Ronald. His tastes run far more plebeian than mine."

Who the hell are these people?

Murphy tried not to gawk at the couple. He desperately avoided his brother's gaze, afraid they'd both burst out laughing. "Why don't we let Maisie give you two a—"

"Oh, no." Ella delicately folded the handkerchief and stowed it in her purse. "One does prefer to spend time with a businessman than the help."

The help?

The help.

"Maisie happens to be one of the two people in charge of the pub and my sister-in-law." Murphy was prepared to put up with a fair amount of nonsense from customers. It was par for the course when dealing with the public. He refused to allow someone to denigrate anyone who worked with him. "Even if she wasn't both of those things, she would still deserve respect, as does everyone you might place in the *help* category."

"One—"

"One should enjoy a tour from these two while I get back to work making mead." Murphy spun around and strode back into the brewery, allowing the door to shut firmly behind him. He chuckled when he spotted Teagan and George practically glued to the window. "Enjoy the show?"

"What a pair of absolute arseholes." Teagan said what Murphy had been thinking. They turned away from the window. "Well, one must get back to work, mustn't one?"

"One must." George snickered. They all had another laugh before pulling themselves together. "Bumble's in your office, sleeping on a blanket if you're wondering. We didn't want his fur getting anywhere near the equipment or mead."

"All right, let's get to experimenting."

FOUR

GEORGE

IT HAD BEEN A ROUGH NIGHT FOR GEORGE. His anxiety and excitement about a date with Murphy had made it impossible to settle down. He'd done a workout, tried a calming tea, and even tried ASMR videos on YouTube, but nothing helped him fall asleep.

What was he going to wear? Should he take his headphones? What about Bumble? He didn't want to subject the poor dog to a wild night at the pub.

Though, wild might be a slight exaggeration. Things never got too loud at the pub. It wasn't large enough, and Murphy ran a tight ship.

Thankfully.

George grabbed his phone and sent his cousin Margo a quick text message. She responded with an affirmative almost immediately. "What do you think, Bumble? Would you like to spend the evening with your auntie?"

Floating through the day in an anxious haze, George finally left the cottage an hour before the tasting. He drove down the lane to his cousin's house. Bumble adored Margo's place; his best friend Treacle lived there.

Treacle was a timid Chihuahua that spent most of his time asleep by the fireplace. Bumble enjoyed being cosy with him. The two had been fast friends since they met.

"There you two are." Margo stepped out of her cottage with a floury apron on. She opened her door all the way to allow Bumble to amble inside to find his friend. "Don't you look handsome?"

"Margo." George hadn't really dressed up. He had changed his usual long-sleeved T-shirt for a button-down and his jeans for trousers. "Sure you don't want to come with?"

"Who's going to watch the children?" Margo glanced back over her shoulder. "They're already curled up in the dog bed. Plus, Maisie told me Ella Donelson would be there. I'd frankly rather eat glass than spend a minute with her and her dreadful husband."

"One would." George dodged back out of reach when she flicked her kitchen towel at her. "Want me to come by after or in the morning?"

"Come in the morning. These scones I'm baking will make for a great brekkie while you spill the details on your date." She tucked the towel into the pocket of her apron. "Just jam your headphones on and avoid the loathsome duo. You'll be all right."

"That should make for an interesting first date."

"Not a first date, Buzz." Margo stepped out of the doorway and came over, resting a comforting hand on his arm. "You're dipping your toes in the pool with the safety of other people around you."

"How is being around other people supposed to relax me?"

"Just... try to enjoy yourself, okay? If you get stressed, Murphy'll let you hide in his office. He always does." Margo squeezed his arm again, then sent him on his way. "Have a pint for me."

There wouldn't actually be pints. Tastings at the brewery tended to involve little glasses of all varieties and whatever little nibbles Maisie had put together. She was a wizard at creating an appetiser menu that paired with the mead.

The parking area in front of the brewery was jam-packed. George slipped on his noise-cancelling headphones before he got out of the vehicle. He adjusted the level to low in the hopes of dimming the overwhelming background noise but still being able to hear conversations.

Honey Bear Brewery had an almost stereotypical Scottish pub attached to it. Wooden panels on the walls and soft lighting made for a warm, cosy atmosphere. Small round tables were littered around the room.

The bar itself took up most of the wall across from the door. They only stocked mead, so glasses lined the shelves instead of the usual liquor bottles. Stools at the counter were already filled with the regulars who came to tastings.

People came to Murphy's place to try the mead on tap that evening and for stories. His grandda and da brought guitars with them. They'd sing and weave tales about the village and other local lore.

Tonight had been different so far. Half of the crowd were the usual locals. The rest were acquaintances of the Donelsons, none of whom seemed thrilled to be there.

The sneering and tittering laughter had begun to rattle George's nerves. He reached up to raise the level of his noise-cancelling headphones. It helped a little, though not much.

"All right, Buzz?" Maisie waved him over. She was pouring water into one of the bowls containing dry ice. "Thought we'd add a bit of atmosphere to the evening."

"Nice." George watched the bubbling, creeping clouds burbling up out of the bowl. "Careful it doesn't get into the mead. Dry ice can be deadly."

Moving across the room, George tried to find Murphy. For a tall bear of a man, he could vanish in the crowd. Instead, he heard someone behind him, though the voice was too muffled to understand.

"How dare you ignore me." Ronald Donelson snatched the headphones off George's head, yanking his long hair in the process. "I asked a question."

"Oi." Murphy thundered his way across the room, shouldering through people who parted like the Red Sea. "Leave him alone, or I'll toss you out on your arse. And keep your bloody hands to yourself."

"I beg your pardon."

"Good. You should." Murphy led George away from Ronald. He paused to grab the headphones before continuing across the pub. "Are you okay?"

George reached up to rub his head, which still smarted a bit from his hair being yanked. "I'm fine. Margo did warn me they were a loathsome duo."

"How about you hide out in my office? I've got a

book I've been meaning to share with you. Tasting should wrap up soon enough." Murphy guided him through the door behind the bar, which led them into the brewery. "Maybe not an ideal first date."

"Margo said this was more of a pre-date. A date teaser." George rested a hand on Murphy's forearm. He hesitated before grasping Murphy by the forearms and leaning up for a kiss. A soft first kiss. A little awkward when their noses bumped together, but they adjusted quickly. "So, where's this book?"

"I'll show you." Murphy cleared his throat a few times. Finally, he flipped the lights on and grabbed a book from behind his desk. "Saw this at a car boot sale a few weeks ago."

"*British Bees: An Introduction to the Study of the Natural History and Economy of the Bees Indigenous to the British Isles.*" George ran a hand reverently across the weathered cover. He traced the gold embossed bee on the front. "I've been hunting for this for ages. It's hard to find the first edition. Bee history is a niche interest."

"Enjoy." Murphy gently placed the noise-cancelling headphones onto George's head. "I'll be back."

He was deep into the first section when a scream jolted him out of his reading. He ripped off his headphones, wondering if he'd misheard. A second blood-curdling yell sent him racing for the bar.

The room was in utter chaos. Several people were shouting into their phones to 999. George pushed through a small cluster to find Graeme on the floor trying to revive Ronald Donelson, whose lips were already turning blue.

"Breathe, Ronald, breathe." Ella spun towards Murphy, swatting him on the arm with her purse. "You did this. You killed him with your frothing drink. You murdered my Ronnie."

FIVE

MURPHY

THE CACOPHONY OF SOUND WAS HORRENDOUS and never-ending. Murphy fended off the assault from a hysterical Ella Donelson. Several of her friends gathered her up and guided her away from the scene. At the same time, the recently arrived paramedics attempted to save her husband's life.

Graeme had trained and worked as a volunteer firefighter, so he had first aid and CPR basics. He'd done his best with Ronald. But, one look at him had told Murphy the man was beyond help.

Ella's screeching didn't calm down until one of the paramedics gave her a sedative. She was led away to the waiting ambulance. Her accusations about the frothing drink had caught the attention of the local constable, who called in one of the detectives from the Major Investigations Team that covered Moray County.

The sinking feeling in his belly only grew worse with each passing moment. Everyone at the tasting had been separated and told not to speak to each other. A forensics team was on the way while the constables sealed off the pub in preparation for the detective.

After what felt like ages, a familiar vehicle pulled into the parking lot. Murphy didn't know whether to sigh in relief or groan in frustration. He knew immediately which of the MIT detectives had been assigned to this case.

"Well, well, well. What have you gotten yourself into this time, Paddington?" DCI Sarah Baird's brown eyes twinkled with amusement when she spotted him. "You can relax, Constable Davie. My cousin's not going anywhere, not if he knows what's good for him. Can you check to see if they're ready to remove the body?"

"Will do." Sean Davie returned to the bar, leaving the two cousins.

"What the devil happened, Paddy?" Sarah crouched down in front of where he was sitting.

With a sigh, Murphy gave her a recounting of the entire evening. He left nothing out—not even his brief flare-up with the deceased. Maisie had served the drinks, so he hadn't touched the glass at any point.

"We both know Maisie wouldn't hurt a fly. So, what happened here? Why was the drink frothing?" Sarah followed his gaze to where he was watching her partner speaking with someone else across the car park. "Murphy?"

"He knows George is autistic, right? So he might not respond the way you expect." Murphy worried they might misunderstand a facial expression, the tone of George's voice, or the lack thereof. He went to move towards them, but his cousin grabbed his arm to stop him. "Sarah?"

"I'm sorry, Paddington. I think this is a conversation we need to have on the record—and I'm not sure a family member should be the one asking the questions. It's a clear conflict of interest." She closed her little notebook and slid it into her pocket. "C'mon. Are you still friends with that solicitor in Keith? We'll be taking you to the station there."

"Sarah." Murphy thought it was a little early for him to be taken in for questioning. "I had nothing to do with this."

"Your bar. Your mead. The way the drink was described sounded like dry ice. Maybe it was an accident. We're bringing in Maisie and Graeme as well. We're just asking questions. That's our job." Sarah began guiding him towards the vehicle she'd arrived in. "Can Teagan stay to lock up once forensics are finished?"

A worried-looking Teagan nodded. They'd been standing close enough to hear what was happening. Murphy asked them to call their mutual friend Evan Chan, the solicitor.

"What's going on?" George deftly stepped around the detective constable who'd been asking him questions. "What are you doing? Are you arresting him? For what? He'd never hurt anyone."

"Easy, George. It's okay. They just have a few questions for me. They're bringing Maisie and Graeme as well. I'm sure it's all standard for an investigation like this one." Murphy tried to ease George's concerns. He wasn't entirely sure any of this was normal. "I'll be fine. Tea's going to call my solicitor. We'll get this all sorted out."

From the worried frown, George didn't believe him. Murphy didn't have time for much more of a conversation. Sarah was waiting impatiently by her vehicle, and the last thing they needed was to create a scene.

They were already being watched.

"Well, if nothing else, we've had a memorable first date." Murphy winked at him and then got into the back seat of his cousin's vehicle. He forced himself to take a few deep breaths. He hadn't done anything; he had to stay calm and answer honestly after speaking with a solicitor. "Sarah? How bad is it?"

"Your bar. Your mead. You had an argument with the deceased, who'd physically attacked your date. The dry ice. It's not brilliant, Murphy." Sarah fell silent when her partner finally joined them. "I think it would be wise to wait until we're on the record for further questions."

The twenty-minute drive to Keith gave Murphy enough time to think through the evening. He started at the beginning, mentally taking himself through everything he remembered. Several people had to have seen him when Ronald received his drink; he hadn't been near it.

That, more than anything else, would likely be his saving grace. If he wasn't near the glass, he couldn't have dropped chunks of dry ice into it. Granted, the police likely had no concrete proof for what had killed Ronald this early.

I didn't do it. I couldn't have. All I have to do is make sure they know it.

SIX

GEORGE

WHILE TEAGAN CALLED EVAN, GEORGE TRIED TO calm his nerves and clear his mind. But whatever Murphy claimed, the police had taken him in for questioning. That was never a good sign.

Ever.

Noticing a couple mid-argument off to the side, George tried to inch closer without being spotted. They'd been part of the group with the Donelsons. He wanted to hear what they were talking about.

George had watched enough true crime to know the first hours of the investigation mattered. He also knew the killer had likely been someone Ronald knew. If it hadn't been an accident. *Maisie's too careful for this to have not been on purpose.*

C'mon, just a little closer.

39

The shadows of the building allowed him to keep out of sight. The couple were ramping up into an impressive shouting match. George kept the noise-cancellation off on his headphones.

"Darren. Her husband just died."

"I'm only saying the bitch hated him. No one believes her dramatics were real. How many times did we hear Ella complain about Ronald? She didn't want to divorce him since he controlled the money." Darren seemed to consider himself quite the authority in the conversation.

"You're daft. The Donelson money goes to his younger brother if he dies, not his wife." His girl-friend or wife swatted him lightly on the arm. "Little Bertrand isn't so little anymore. He's home from university and doesn't do much more than lounge around, from what I heard Ella complaining."

"Don't the Donelson brothers hate each other? So why would Bertrand come home? I'd expected him to stay in London enjoying the high life." Darren glanced towards the pub but didn't seem to see George. "Are you sure you heard right, Natalia?"

"I did. Besides, wouldn't you hate the person who controls the majority of your inheritance? Ella said Ronnie threatened to cut off the allowance from his trust if he didn't stop carousing around

London." Natalia was interrupted by her phone beeping. "Why don't we head to the hospital? Maybe they'll let us talk to her to find out what happened."

Pressing himself tighter against the outer wall of the pub, George held his breath when they walked past him. Thankfully, they didn't glance in his direction. Instead, he waited until they'd gone to speak to the police before returning to where Teagan stood.

"Well? What'd you hear?" Teagan asked once he'd snuck back over to them. "Anything interesting?"

George gave her a brief recap of the conversations he'd overheard. "Should we tell the police?"

"Not sure what exactly we have that we could tell them? You overheard gossiping." Teagan shrugged. "Why don't we see if they'll let us leave?"

The police, after getting their information, allowed them to leave. Teagan had already locked up the pub. The forensic team had wrapped up; they'd taken the glass, the mead, and security footage from all of the cameras in and around the brewery.

Arriving home, George sat outside of his cottage for several minutes. It was dark inside. He couldn't bring himself to get out of the vehicle.

It was two in the morning. But George made a

three-point turn and drove the short distance to Margo's cottage instead. He didn't want to be alone.

Not after the night he'd had.

He was haunted by having watched the life go out of Ronald's face. His blue lips. The way his eyes went blank. The bloodcurdling scream from Ella. Everything was so overwhelming that he found his hands still trembling hours later.

Pulling up in front of her cottage, George took a few shaky breaths. He turned off the engine and somehow managed to get the keys out. His fingers fumbled with the buckle on the seat belt before finally releasing it.

George wanted a warm mug of tea, biscuits, and puppy cuddles. He was surprised to see several lights on. The door opened when he was halfway up the path to the cottage. "Margo."

"Rough night, Buzz?" She opened her arms and waited for him to decide if he wanted a hug. He hesitated, then stepped into her embrace. She gently patted his back. "Why don't we pop into the kitchen, lovely? I've got a fresh pot of tea just about ready. I have some of Baba's shortbread biscuits that you love so much. Everything's going to be right as rain. You'll see."

"Is it? How's your dad doing anyway?" George

followed her into the cottage. He stopped when he spotted Bumble and Treacle curled up around each other in a large, fluffy dog bed. "Isn't that too big for your Chihuahua?"

"Treacle thinks he's a much larger dog. And Baba's fine, complaining I don't visit him enough." Margo went straight into the kitchen. She set out two mugs and puttered around, getting the tea ready. "Disrupt Prince Treacle's sleep at your own risk. He doesn't like to be woken up."

Crouching down by the dogs, George lightly patted Bumble on the head. He smiled at the rumbling snores from his pug. The familiar snuffling soothed some of the anxiety from the chaotic evening.

"George?"

He gave one last scratch to Bumble, then stood up. "Yeah?"

"Tea's ready." Margo had set everything up on the little kitchen table. She had a little plate filled with sweet treats and a few sandwiches. "I wasn't sure if you'd gotten to eat before everything went tits up."

"Not sure I'm hungry."

"Have a sip of tea," Margo encouraged. She

dropped a sugar cube into her mug and slowly stirred. "Do you want to talk about it?"

"Maybe." George wrapped his fingers around the mug. "Evan Chan texted me. They've still got Murphy at the police station in Keith."

"He'll be okay. Evan's a good solicitor. Dedicated to his clients. You know he'll make sure your Murphy's fine." Margo stretched her arm out to grab his hand, squeezing it before letting go. "Sip your tea. It'll make you feel better."

"It'll make me feel warm and caffeinated."

"Like I said, it'll make you feel better." Margo bit into one of the chocolate-covered shortbreads. "Try a biscuit. You've had a shock; some sugar will do you good."

With a dutiful sigh, George grabbed one of the flower-shaped biscuits. They were pistachio and saffron shortbread with a drizzle of white chocolate. It was sweet, buttery, and perfect.

Over shortbread and tea, George shared the events of the day. He told her about his brief altercation with Ronald Donelson and the man's terrible, gasping breaths on the pub floor. She perked up when he mentioned the conversation he'd overheard.

"Darren and Natalia?" Margo reached out for another biscuit.

"You know them?"

"I used to work with Darren before the accident." Margo had been a paramedic until she'd been involved in a horrific accident in her ambulance. A drunk driver had ploughed into them at a high rate of speed, sending them careening off the road. She'd been in a coma for weeks and had suffered from post-traumatic stress ever since. "I trained him. We rode together for months."

"He was a paramedic? So why didn't he try to help Ronald?" George recalled seeing the man on the edge of the crowd around the prone body on the floor. "Graeme was the only person who did."

"Now, that's an interesting question. Darren and Ella were always quite close."

"How close?" George nibbled on the shortbread. He was suddenly taken back to his last visit with their grandfather. "You sure this was your dad's recipe? Tastes a little more like Dada Ji's."

"This is definitely my baba's recipe. He adds more pistachio." Margo leaned forward with her elbows on the table. "Back to Darren and Ella. They were way too close. I heard all sorts of rumours."

"Yeah?" George glared at his cousin when she continued to draw things out. "Quit being unnecessarily dramatic."

"Fine, fine. Several of the other paramedics swore they'd seen them kissing."

"And?" George wiped his fingers on the kitchen towel on the table. "Kissing can be completely innocent."

"Not when his tongue was halfway down her throat."

"Don't think that's physically possible." George sipped his tea. "Does he have an unusually long tongue?"

"I meant metaphorically."

"How does one metaphorically shove... never mind." George decided the details didn't matter. The detailed explanation would only frustrate him. "Did you know dry ice could kill someone?"

"Technically, yes? In layman's terms, a small chunk of dry ice could stick in your oesophagus. It not only causes damage but produces carbon dioxide. You run the risk of choking to death. It can be deadly or simply do damage to your throat. There's a danger if it gets into your stomach." Margo went into a more detailed explanation, but George was stuck on the first part. "You're not listening."

"Carbon dioxide poisoning." George pushed the plate of shortbread away. He'd suddenly lost his appetite. "So either we have a true accident, which I don't believe. None of the drinks at the party included dry ice. It was left in a cauldron on the bar counter. Anyone could've accessed it."

"Or, it was no accident."

"Exactly. We know Maisie, Graeme, and Murphy had nothing to do with it." George would bet his entire life on the three being innocent of all wrongdoing. "So, someone else in the pub chipped some dry ice into the glass and gave it to Ronald."

"Small gathering means only a few suspects." Margo leaned back in her chair, pulling open a drawer in the kitchen and grabbing a notebook. She found a pen as well. "We should get organised."

"Organised?"

"You're going to poke your nose into this investigation, Buzz. I know you. You're as obsessed with true crime as I am. They've taken Murphy, the love of your life, in for questioning." Margo grinned when he grumbled at her choice of words. "So? Who are the prime suspects?"

"Are you going to help me?"

"Every Sherlock needs a Watson to keep him out of trouble." Margo tapped her pen against the paper. "We're putting Ella and Darren at the top."

"And Ronald's brother."

"Ella, Bertrand, and Darren." Margo jotted down the three names on separate pages.

"Well, it's a place to start." George watched her grab her phone and send a message. "It's three in the morning. No one's going to be awake."

"A person died at the brewery. I guarantee you far more people are awake than you think. Tiny village? Big gossips." Margo smirked when her phone began to chirp and vibrate on the table. "I'll have everything but their bank account information in less than an hour."

"Local gossip is always more effective than a police inquiry."

"Though maybe not always as accurate," Margo conceded.

"Then what? You get potentially faulty information from your local sources? We can't traipse around the village asking questions." George had to reconsider for a second. It wasn't the worst idea Margo had ever had. "Could we?"

"If you're not playing Sherlock, how can I be Watson?"

SEVEN

MURPHY

Two things kept Murphy calm in the interrogation room while detectives threw questions at him. First, the pub had security cameras. Second, he hadn't touched the glass involved in the incident.

Evan sat beside him through all of it. He offered the police multiple witnesses who placed Murphy away from the victim and his drink. "Face it, Detectives. He has no motive. Several people within the pub and the CCTV footage point to him being on the opposite side of the room. You're wasting your time with my client."

The two detective constables exchanged glances. DC Smith reached out to stop the recording. They closed their notebooks, allowing Murphy to finally relax into the uncomfortable chair.

"We're inclined to agree with you. But witnesses also indicated Mr Baird had an argument with the deceased within an hour of the victim's death," DC Jones pointed out. "However, the footage clearly shows he had no opportunity to put the dry ice into the drink. So you're free to go."

It felt like "for now" lingered in the air unspoken. They couldn't pin the crime on him. But Murphy couldn't help thinking they hadn't removed him from their list of suspects.

When they finally stepped outside to find the sun had risen, the sky was a riot of colour. Beautiful oranges, yellows, and pinks. Murphy inhaled deeply, enjoying the cool breeze against his skin. He tilted his head back to stare up at the clouds passing by.

"You okay, Paddy?" Evan moved up beside him. He had his briefcase at his side. "It's a little after four. Fancy a coffee and some breakfast? Or do you just want me to drive you straight home?"

"Let me text everyone. Let them know I'm all right." Murphy sent the same message to Teagan, his brother, and George. He was surprised when the latter responded almost instantly. Finally, he glanced over at Evan. "How about an early morning brekkie with Buzz and Margo?"

"You still embarrassing yourself by how in love you are with our bee bloke?"

"You still terrified of Margo and your feelings for her?" Murphy dodged the briefcase being swung at him. "Careful. They might arrest you for assault."

"Let's get out of here before both of us wind up being asked questions again." Evan led him across the street to where his car was parked. "Margo won't mind me crashing your breakfast?"

"Margo made the invitation to both of us." Murphy squashed himself into the passenger seat of Evan's little hatchback. "Why do you insist on driving this clown car?"

"You could walk."

With a grin at his friend, Murphy tried to make himself more comfortable. Unfortunately, he felt like an extra-large sardine squashed into a tiny tin. Evan just snickered at him and continued driving.

Evan Chan had lived in Keith his entire life. Murphy had known him for years. They were the same age and had gone to the same school until he'd left for university.

"You ever regret not staying in Edinburgh? You'd probably make more money." Murphy had been surprised when Evan returned home. "There have to be better opportunities for a solicitor in a bigger city."

"And miss helping arbitrate cases about lost sheep? I'm never bored." Evan shrugged. "Plus, my parents are getting older. They were struggling. I'm the oldest. It's on me to make sure they're taken care of."

"How's Celeste doing?"

"Off in Australia at the moment. She's got the lead in a play. Think she's going to be there for at least another six months." Evan had moved into his parents' home to take care of them. It had put a damper on his ability to date. "She has a new girlfriend. They're blissfully happy. I might vomit."

"Are we done being overly cheerful to distract ourselves?" Murphy picked at a piece of fluff on his jeans. "They almost arrested me for murder."

"They questioned you. Nothing out of the ordinary. I wouldn't go so far as to say you were almost arrested." Evan was ever the voice of reason when it came to things related to the law. "Have you been watching true crime docs again?"

"Evan."

"They're intimidating on purpose, Murphy. They want to catch you out in a lie. That's why you have a solicitor with you—to protect your rights." Evan paused before pulling into the sparse early morning traffic. "If they'd had enough to arrest you, the conversation would've gone quite differently."

"They questioned me like they thought I'd killed the man."

"A man died in your pub from something in your mead. You'd had an argument with him earlier that was witnessed by everyone present." Evan waxed on for a few minutes as if he worked for the crown prosecution. "They had to ask you uncomfortable questions. I doubt they seriously considered you as a suspect, particularly after seeing the CCTV footage."

"Easy to say from your seat," Murphy grumbled. He felt a little put out at having obviously been an unwilling participant in a little legal theatrics. "They didn't have to make me feel like I'd killed the man."

"A man died. They're doing their job. Now, if they'd actually tried to arrest you, I'd take issue with them." Evan gave another indifferent shrug. "You're tired and hungry. The night was ruined, along with your first date. You've a right to a good sulk."

"Not sulking."

"You are one hundred percent sulking. It's not attractive, so don't let George see you." Evan laughed when Murphy muttered curses under his breath. "I promise my parents were definitely married when they had me."

Deciding to finish his sulking in silence, Murphy stared out the window. The bright oranges and yellows had shifted into more muted colours as the sun rose higher in the sky. It was going to be a lovely morning.

It was too bad Murphy felt like he'd been run over by a lorry—twice. The day would've been a brilliant reason to ask George out for a walk. They could've taken Bumble with them. Instead, all he wanted now was a warm mug of tea, a hearty breakfast, and a long nap, preferably in that order.

"Wake up, grumpy. We're here." Evan nudged his arm a few times. "Murphy?"

"I heard you." Murphy hadn't even realised he'd fallen asleep until Evan had called his name. "I'm exhausted."

"Oh, hello." Evan's words came out in a hushed whisper. His attention was on the cottage in front of them. "Do I look all right?"

"You look like I woke you up at two in the morning and dragged you down to the police station." Murphy tried not to laugh when Evan hurriedly adjusted his tie and dragged his fingers through his hair. "I doubt Margo will even notice, given the time of morning."

"That's even worse. She won't even notice if I look good or not." Evan had gone from a crisp, put-together solicitor into a panicking mess in the blink of an eye. "Murphy."

"I am too tired to handle your existential crisis. Not sure Margo's looking for a relationship or a date." Murphy opened the door and dragged himself out of the clown car with a little effort. He wound up practically rolling out of the vehicle onto the ground. "I can hear you laughing at me."

"That was not a graceful exit by any stretch of the imagination." Margo snickered at him.

"Not my fault Evan has a matchbox car." Murphy pushed himself up to his feet. He dusted off his jeans and stretched for a second. "Morning."

"Sun's up. Definitely morning. There are eggs, bacon, beans, and crumpets. A fresh pot of tea, or I've got coffee if you prefer." Margo gave him a quick hug. "Go on inside. My poor cousin's spent all night worried about you."

"All night?" Murphy tried not to grin at the admission.

"You're both fools. Go on." Margo turned her attention to Evan. "Ah, the solicitor general."

"Joke hasn't been funny any of the times you've said it," Evan stammered, much to Murphy's amusement. He stayed by the door, watching the man stumble over their conversation. "Paddington."

"Going inside. Going inside." Murphy winked at Margo when she turned to glare at him. "He likes you. Let him down gently. I'd hate to have to find a new solicitor and friend."

Making his way into the cottage, Murphy was greeted by the scrambling of nails on the hardwood floor. He crouched down to catch Bumble and Treacle when they raced to get to him. They greeted him enthusiastically, helping to wipe away the wretchedness he'd felt most of the long night at the police station.

"Have you been behaving yourselves?" Murphy gathered the two dogs into his arms. He managed to stand up while carefully juggling them. "Did you have brekkie?"

"You're free." George skidded to a stop, having raced back into the cottage from the garden. "I had this terrifying thought they'd change their minds. Want some tea?"

"I just want to sit for a minute." Murphy thought his legs might actually give out on him. He sank onto Margo's plush old couch, setting the dogs on the cushion beside him. Bumble immediately curled up in his lap while Treacle clambered up on the top of the sofa and plopped down on his shoulder. "I'm stuck in, it seems."

"I'll join you." George kicked off his shoes and moved to sit beside him, twisting around to stretch his legs out and make himself comfortable against Murphy's side. "You all right, Paddington?"

"Not how I'd hoped to end our date."

"You weren't expecting a dead body and police investigation?" George's laugh had a slight edge to it. "What did you hope for?"

"A quiet moment together once the pub was empty." Murphy hadn't necessarily had a plan for what might happen next. "Not spending my evening being bombarded with questions by stone-faced detectives."

"Later, when I'm not half asleep, remind me to tell you what Margo and I put together." George shuffled a little beside him. His long hair tickled Murphy's neck. "We were going to storm the castle."

"What castle?" Murphy didn't get an answer. George slumped further against him, and his breathing evened out. He'd obviously fallen asleep. "Never mind, Buzz. Get some rest."

Closing his eyes, Murphy allowed himself to

relax for the first time in several long hours. He adjusted his arm, so it was wrapped around George. Treacle moved from his neck and curled up beside Bumble.

He was sure they made quite a sight. Margo was going to have a field day when she saw them. He cracked an eye open, surprised to find Evan and his crush were still outside.

Interesting.

He hoped Margo was letting poor Evan down gently.

Murphy dared not move. The two dogs and George were a symphony of snoring around him. *Not the worst way to end our date.*

It wasn't silent in the cosy comfort of Margo's cottage. Napping with a pug could never be considered quiet. Bumble's snoring mingled with Treacle's. It was sweet.

"Oh, oh they're adorable. Get a photo."

The sound of hushed whispers woke Murphy up. He hadn't even realised he'd drifted off to sleep. The voices and footsteps came closer; he could hear the sound of someone taking a photo with their phone.

Probably Margo.

"Aren't they sweet?" Margo had definitely

moved closer. He heard the click of another photo. "I have to send these to his parents. Oh my—"

"I can hear you." George surprised Murphy by speaking.

Murphy helped George sit up. The two dogs continued to snooze away in his lap. "What were you two doing outside for so long?"

"Not snoozing on the couch in a little cuddle pile." Margo heaved a sigh. She set her phone on a nearby table. "Why don't we all have some breakfast? I'm sure you three are more than ready for a lengthy nap. Some food will do you good."

Treacle dashed off his lap immediately when Margo and Evan moved towards the kitchen. Bumble was more lackadaisical. George reached out to lift him up and set him on the ground, which made the pug quite put out if the grunting was any sign.

"Don't be sassy, Bumble. Brekkie doesn't magically appear in front of you." George frowned. "Though, I suppose it does from your perspective."

Murphy always loved how George had entire conversations with his dog. "Maybe breakfast will magically appear for all of us if we migrate into the kitchen."

"Or, you can migrate to the kitchen and give me a hand with what I'd already made. Tea definitely needs redoing. No one likes an over-stewed brew." Margo grabbed the pot off the round table, emptying it into the sink. "Let me get the kettle going again. George? You awake enough to pop some crumpets into the toaster?"

"How awake does one have to be?" George asked with a grin.

"Less snark, more crumpets."

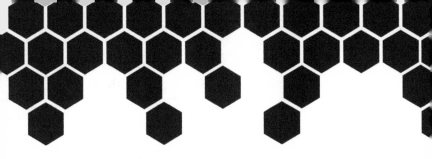

EIGHT

GEORGE

Breakfast had been quieter than George expected. Instead, they'd all found themselves exhausted. The late night (or early morning) had caught up with all four of them.

Margo had clung to her mug of tea, nodding off in her chair. George had told her to head off to bed, promising to clean up for her. Murphy had helped after Evan left; he'd ordered them to keep him updated on any changes.

They let the dogs run in the back garden, then locked things up for Margo. George fished in his pocket for his keys and leaned tiredly against his beat-up old Range Rover.

"So, what are you planning for our second date?" He closed his eyes to relieve some of the itchiness.

They were dry and gritty. He wanted nothing more than to splash warm water on his face and then sink into his bed for the rest of the day. "Are we going to find ourselves in the middle of a bank robbery or something as an encore?"

"It'd feel no less dramatic." Murphy came over to lean next to him. Bumble sat at their feet, happily panting away and watching a butterfly flitting around the front garden. "You never did tell us what you and Margo had been doing."

"Why don't we get some sleep first? Everything will make more sense when I haven't been up for twenty-four hours." George was sure anything he said at this point would be as clear as mud. "How about I give you a ride back to the brewery?"

"You sure you're awake enough? You've got a couch. Mind if I crash on it?"

"Probably safer than risking a car accident because we're so sodding tired." George was almost tempted to walk, but he wasn't sure he had the energy for it. "Come on, Bumble. Time to go home."

The short drive to the cottage was uneventful. George barely managed a wave in the direction of the couch before collapsing onto his bed. He didn't even take off his shoes; he was asleep before his head had fully touched the pillow.

From the sun's position through the window, George knew he'd slept longer than expected. He grabbed his phone off the nightstand to confirm it was just gone noon. Poor Bumble was probably ready to burst.

Scrambling out of bed, George rushed into the living room to find Bumble and Murphy sharing a sandwich. They both seemed quite content. He stumbled to a halt and stared at them.

"He wake you up?"

"Thought he was going to lick my nose off." Murphy offered Bumble a little sliver of ham. "Graeme and Maisie brought sandwiches along with my vehicle. There's a whole plate of these in the fridge. I took your little one for a walk, since he seemed desperate for the garden."

"Probably was." George rubbed his eyes to get the sleep out of them. He noticed the tall cup on the table in front of him. "Is that a cold brew?"

"Yep." Murphy smirked at him. "There's one in the fridge for you. Strawberry cream cold brew, just how you like it. Apparently, the barista knew you by name?"

"They know Bumble. Not me." George went to the Dufftown café at least once a week. They had a bowl especially for his dog and always filled it with whipped cream for him. "He's a rock star. I'm just the minion who lugs him around."

"At least you know your place." Murphy laughed when Bumble placed a paw on his leg and nudged the plate in his hand. "How much can he have?"

"He's probably already had enough." George went into the kitchen to find the plate and, more importantly, his strawberry cream cold brew. He took a long sip, finishing with a very satisfied smile. "I suddenly feel human again."

"All it took was berries, cream, and caffeine?"

"And sleep." George sat on the arm of the couch. He continued to sip on the coffee. "Did Graeme and Maisie have any news? Aside from being the bearers of gifts."

"No arrests. Lots of rumours about my being locked up. Ella Donelson is out of the hospital and telling everyone I killed her beloved husband." Murphy finished the last bite of his sandwich. He dusted his fingers off then placed the empty plate on the coffee table. "He saw the security footage before turning it over to the police."

"And?"

"It clears me, Maisie, and Graeme but doesn't show who put the dry ice in the glass," Murphy said with a frustrated groan. "So, the police don't have a smoking gun."

"Or smoking ice?" George took a bite of the sandwich half that he'd grabbed from the fridge. "Someone in the pub had to have done it."

"That is correct."

"And it wasn't either of you three. I certainly didn't do it. We have a short list of people who could be involved." George thought about what he and Margo had worked out the night—or morning—before. "I know where we could start."

"Start?"

"Start trying to solve the murder." George set his coffee down. He found a tie in his pocket and drew his hair into a ponytail. "How hard can it be?"

"George."

"What?" George searched his pockets before finding the paper with his notes. "We're going to figure out who did this. My bet is on the brother or the lover."

"I..." Murphy paused for the briefest moment. "Wait. What? Who?"

While finishing his coffee and sandwich, George updated Murphy on all the local gossip Margo had shared. It did seem a little absurd to get stuck into a police investigation. But he couldn't get the image of the detectives leading Murphy away out of his head.

"What about the wife?"

"Also on the top of my list."

"A three-horse race, then?" Murphy took the paper when George offered it to him. He skimmed through the thoughts they'd jotted down. "We could turn this over to the police."

"We could." George became fascinated with his empty cup. He counted the ice, trying not to show his disappointment.

"Or we could poke around the village. Ask a few questions." Murphy tapped his finger against the paper. "You've made a good start. All three of them have a motive. First, though, we should see if an affair was actually happening."

"True. Margo said paramedics gossip a fair bit."

"Everyone does. We're doing it now." Murphy folded the paper and handed it back to him. "Tell you what. The brewery's going to be closed for a few days because of the police inquiry. How about I head home for a shower and a change of clothes, then we take a walk through the village? See if anyone wants to chat with us?"

"A second date with a side of murder mystery?"

"I'd hate to be boring." Murphy chuckled.

NINE

MURPHY

THE MAGNITUDE OF WHAT HAPPENED DIDN'T HIT Murphy fully until he stood in the shower. With hot water pelting him in the face, he allowed himself to work through the flood of emotions. A man had died in his pub, and he'd been considered potentially responsible.

A man had died. Or, to be more accurate, he had been murdered. Ronald Donelson had been an absolute arsehole, but he hadn't deserved to go out on a pub floor.

The heat of the water helped clear away some of the lingering anxiety. But, despite Evan's confidence, Murphy had been genuinely concerned. The incident did happen in his brewery, and he'd had an altercation with the man.

With no other information, Murphy might've suspected himself. He thanked his lucky stars he'd taken his brother's advice to install cameras outside and inside. It had likely saved him a wealth of trouble.

Murphy finally turned the water off. *Sarah's going to kill me when she finds out we're playing detective.*

His cousin had a dim view of private investigators. She'd likely not appreciate amateur detectives either. He decided not to worry about it.

Not today, anyway.

Today, Murphy planned to have a less eventful second date with George. Less murder, more conversation and kissing. Though, if they were going to ask questions, it wouldn't be without at least a hint of the macabre.

A few hours later, Murphy had showered and changed. He'd chatted with his dad and granddad, reassuring them he hadn't been thrown into solitary confinement. Teagan had also called to check in on him; they'd offered to meet up with him in the village.

The grey skies suited his mood when Murphy finally ventured outside. His lips twitched in amusement when he spotted George and Bumble walking towards him. The latter had a wee raincoat on him, complete with a hat.

"Did you dress up for the date, Bumble?" Murphy crouched down to give his chin a scratch. "Aren't you a sight?"

"He doesn't enjoy the rain," George muttered defensively.

"Well, he is closer to the ground." Murphy winked at him and then got to his feet. "I can't say I blame him."

They stood awkwardly for a moment. Murphy waited it out. He didn't want to push George for anything or make him uncomfortable.

George's gaze darted around before landing on Murphy's nose. He lunged forward and grabbed him by the arms. "Kissing is okay? Right?"

"More than." Murphy was impressed by the strength in George's fingers, which held him tightly by the forearms. He bent a little to meet him half-way. "Kissing might become my favourite way to pass the time."

"You're daft." George released him when Bumble complained loudly at them. "Have we ignored you too much?"

"Right. Into the village, we go." Murphy laughed when Bumble gave a little shake and ambled along in front of them. "I'd say he's ready to go."

"It's late enough in the afternoon. I thought we could meander down Balvenie Street. We can pop into the Coffee Pot for a fresh brew. We'll likely run into Darren Fishwick. He'll probably be near the florist, where his wife works." George had obviously put in a fair amount of thought. "Margo's going to see if she can't speak to Ella Donelson. I doubt she'd be amenable to speaking to either of us, particularly since she's still telling anyone who'll listen you killed her husband."

"Maybe don't say that part out loud?" Murphy winced. He knew how rumours flew around a small village. "Here's hoping people know me well enough to know it's a load of shite."

"If they don't, we'll have to prove it to them," George stated quite firmly. He had a fierce look in his eyes. "I'll send my bees after them."

"Do your bees attack on command?"

"I'll figure it out." George nudged him with his elbow. "How hard can it be to make a squadron of attack bees?"

"Not sure it's going to help convince people I'm too mild-mannered to have done this." Murphy threw his arm around George. He couldn't help the little thrill of finally being free to show his affection for the man beside him. Teagan had been right; he was daft for not asking him out sooner. "You've trained them not to attack you."

"Not so much trained them but learned how to be at one with the bees." George purposefully made it sound far more dramatic than it needed to be. They both chuckled for a second. "They're lovely, my little hive monsters. I don't know why people are so afraid of them."

"Stings."

"They only sting if you don't respect them." George adjusted his hold on Bumble's leash, allowing him to lean closer to Murphy. "People are going to suspect we're stepping out."

"Stepping out?"

"The words my auntie used when Margo told her about our first date. I think the exact phrase was, 'he's stepping out with his young man.'" George seemed to find it entertaining.

"Is your auntie perhaps stuck in a time warp?" Murphy dodged around some muck in the road. "Sarah told me to stay out of trouble."

"Okay."

"Sarah also used to eat crayons." Murphy knew she wouldn't necessarily appreciate the reminder.

Detective Constable Baird took herself quite seriously. "I'm not overly concerned about her telling me to stay out of trouble. But, let's not just run up to our suspects and ask if they killed someone."

"We can be subtle." George didn't sound entirely confident. He did struggle at times with being too blunt. He tended to prefer getting straight to the point. "When in doubt, distract them with Bumble. Plus, Margo's already laid some of the groundwork for us. She asked around some of her friends who still work with the ambulance service. One of them confirmed seeing Ella and Darren exchanging more than a friendly peck on the cheek."

"Are you ready to be an accessory, Bumble?" Murphy heard a vehicle coming up the lane behind them. He had a split second to glance over his shoulder before snatching up the pug and dragging George out of the way. They watched it go roaring past them far too quickly for the narrow road. "What the bloody hell were they thinking?"

"Did you get the vehicle registration?"

"Too worried about getting you and Bumble out of the way." Murphy handed Bumble over to George with trembling hands. He knew they'd had an extraordinarily close call. "I recognised the car. It was at the brewery the night of the tasting. Not sure who owns it, but I know I saw it. But why? We haven't even asked any questions."

"Well...."

"George? Talk to me, Buzz."

"I might've asked a few questions on the online community forum." George cuddled Bumble close to his chest. "Subtle ones."

"How subtle?"

"Is there a sliding scale of subtlety?" George was definitely skirting the question. "I asked if anyone had been at the tasting and if they recalled seeing anything out of the ordinary. I might've asked if anyone had video."

"George."

"What? It might prove helpful."

"It also might've told someone you were poking your nose into the murder investigation." Murphy ensured they were both back on solid ground before grabbing his phone. He went to call his cousin, then reconsidered. "I have no idea what to say to Sarah. Some numpty tried to run us over? We've no proof. What would we tell her?"

"A red car with a dent on the side may or may not have purposefully attempted to murder us while we were walking down a narrow lane." George shifted Bumble in his arms to make him more comfortable. "Maybe mention it next time you speak with her?"

Murphy stopped walking to take a better look around. Unfortunately, he didn't see any CCTV cameras. "Shite. I was hoping there'd be a camera."

"There's one around the corner near the football pitch." George took a breath and set a wiggling Bumble down on the ground. "Let's keep walking."

TEN

GEORGE

THE CLOSE ENCOUNTER OF A VEHICULAR KIND had jarred George's nerves. He wanted nothing more than to snatch Bumble off the ground and run back to the safety of his cottage. It was possibly an irrational thought.

Maybe not irrational when he considered how close they'd come.

They eventually made their way to the Coffee Pot. There were a number of people sitting outside, chatting away despite the threat of rain. Murphy waved to a few of them; George focused his attention on Bumble, never sure about greeting those he didn't know well.

Murphy had grown up in Dufftown. Just about

everyone in the village knew him. George was a relatively new face by comparison.

The village had welcomed George with open arms. However, he still struggled at times to get used to the overly friendly greetings. Bumble helped, since everyone adored a snuffling pug in a raincoat.

Who wouldn't?

While doing his level best to avoid making eye contact, George spotted Darren and Natalia across the street in front of the florist. They were having a heated conversation.

Nudging Murphy with his elbow, George tried to casually make his way closer. He allowed Bumble to take the lead. It gave him an excuse for meandering across the street without seeming to eavesdrop on the couple.

"I saw you, Darren. I saw you with that conniving..." Natalia's voice trailed off. George couldn't hear the next bit of the conversation. "You weren't subtle at the pub. Snuggling up like I wasn't in the sodding room. Maybe I should tell the police about how Ella Donelson was shagging you? Miss Prim and Proper having a tawdry affair. Perhaps the detectives should put your name at the top of their list. Where were you when poor old Ronnie choked on ice?"

"Will you shut up?" Darren grabbed her by the

arms, dragging her into her shop and slamming the door closed.

Their voices faded away. George continued past, noticing Darren had flipped the sign from open to closed. *Interesting*. He completed a loop down to the end of the street and then circled back to Murphy, who'd gotten coffees, pastries, and a treat for Bumble.

They chose a table further away from the rest. George offered Bumble the little biscuit along with a bowl of water. He glanced around to ensure no one was paying them any attention.

"Well?"

"Natalia Fishwick's aware of her husband's philandering ways. She threw it in his face and practically accused him of being the one to kill Ronald Donelson." George kept reminding himself to keep his voice low. He wasn't always brilliant with moderating his tone. With a quick sip of coffee and then another cursory glance around him, he continued to tell Murphy what he'd heard. "She might've just been threatening him for cheating."

"Maybe. It's certainly interesting she immediately went there." Murphy leaned in closer. "We're not going to get anything out of them—"

He was cut off by the sound of breaking glass. They twisted around in their chairs to see a vase had been launched through one of the florist shop windows. Darren came rushing outside.

"Well, shite," Murphy muttered.

They watched Natalia chase him out of the shop. She stood on the pavement, breathing heavily and holding a heavy glass vase in her hand. At the same time, Darren vanished around the corner.

"There's definitely trouble in paradise with the Fishwicks." George took a bite of his pastry. He watched while Natalia continued to shout curses. "But did the trouble involve dry ice in a drink?"

"No idea." Murphy gestured with his coffee cup to something behind George. "Am I imagining things, or is Darren driving a suspiciously familiar vehicle?"

"Same colour." George watched it drive by them, checking for damage to the side. "Same dent. It is indeed a *suspiciously* familiar car."

"Get back here, you bastard!"

Everyone at the Coffee Pot twisted around to watch Natalia. She rushed out of her shop and launched a vase at the passing car. Darren wisely sped up until he was out of sight—and reach of her arm.

With a shriek of frustration, Natalia spun around and returned to her shop. The door slammed shut behind her. There was a shocked silence for all of a second before hushed conversations picked up around them.

"Coffee and a show?" Murphy whistled, shaking his head. "Not exactly what I hoped we'd discover if we came into the village."

"Hello, lads." Teagan waved cheerily at them. They grabbed a chair and sat at their little table. "Sorry to crash your coffee date."

"Less of a date, more of a live screening of the latest TV show—Real Housewives of Dufftown." George continued to keep an eye on the floral shop. He could see Natalia on her phone. She was waving her hands around widely. "Not a happy woman. Maybe someone should offer her a sympathetic ear?"

"Not a bad idea. She might be more amenable to answering questions about Darren, Ella, and Ronald." Murphy glanced over at Teagan. "You're a neutral party."

"You say the sweetest things." Teagan rolled their eyes. They grabbed the pastry left on Murphy's plate and scarfed it down in one bite. "Fine. I'll go check on dear Natalia. Here's hoping she remembers my auntie. Maybe I can use it to get myself in the door."

With a beleaguered sigh, Teagan chugged down

the last of their coffee. They made their way across the street and inside the florist. George and Murphy watched through the window.

Natalia seemed hostile at having her private angst intruded upon. It was hard for George to tell from a distance. He'd never been brilliant at reading body language.

"We should stop staring." Murphy nudged his knee to get his attention. "Natalia might notice and realise Teagan's kindness has an ulterior motive."

"It does."

"True, but probably better for Teagan if Natalia doesn't realize it's anything other than perhaps a normal amount of curiosity mixed with concern." Murphy bent down to check on Bumble, who'd stretched out between them. "Belly full of whipped cream. He seems quite pleased with himself."

"Spoilt little monster. Of course he is."

They pretended to focus on their coffee. But really, George knew they were both more interested in the conversation at the florist shop. He had no idea if Natalia would tell Teagan anything at all.

George couldn't help risking a glance across the street to see Teagan exiting the shop. "Conversation appears to be over."

"Longer than I thought it'd be. From Natalia's

mood, I figured she'd kick Teagan out almost immediately." Murphy peered into his coffee cup. "Are you finished?"

"Yep?"

"Why don't we have Teagan give us a lift back to the brewery? We can speak there without anyone listening to our conversation." Murphy gathered up their empty cups and plates. "I'll take care of these."

While Murphy was inside the Coffee Pot, George sent a message to his cousin. Margo immediately invited all three of them over. He figured Teagan and Murphy wouldn't mind. Bumble would be excited to see his best friend as well.

"Everything all right?" Murphy returned just as Teagan made it back to their table.

"Margo's inviting us over to her cottage. She has snacks." George also knew his cousin struggled with loneliness. She'd developed a fear of driving after the accident, so she didn't get out much. "She knew Darren fairly well. Might be able to give us more insight."

"I'm all for snacks," Teagan readily agreed. "Why don't I drive us to the brewery? You can pick up your Range Rover so you don't have to double back later."

When they finally arrived at Margo's, Bumble

was bouncing excitedly. He always recognised when they were getting close to her place. George struggled to get him out of his safety belt with all the wiggling.

"Bumble. Calm yourself." George finally had to set him down. He immediately bolted for the cottage. Margo had already opened the door. Treacle met his best friend halfway up the path, and they danced around each other excitedly. "You'd never know they see each other at least every few days. You'd think it's been weeks or months."

"Days are a really long time in dog years." Margo laughed when Treacle and Bumble ran circles around them before flopping down on their bellies on the grass. "Well, that's them exhausted."

"C'mon, lads, into the house. I'm sure Margo has treats for you." George nudged Bumble lightly with his toe. He didn't budge an inch. "You ran for all of five seconds. You can't possibly be this tired."

With some cajoling, they managed to get everyone into the cottage. Margo had sandwiches and biscuits for them. She'd also gotten a pot of tea brewing. It was the perfect counterpart for them to share their tale.

"She threw a vase at him?" Margo stood frozen,

still pouring tea. Teagan leapt up to grab her arm before the cup overflowed. "Thanks, Tea."

"Happy to help." They blushed.

George noticed how they lingered for a second, Teagan's hand still on Margo's arm. *Interesting.* He glanced over at Murphy, who winked at him. *Right, time to change the subject before things get awkward.* "So, Natalia clearly thinks Darren's capable of killing Ronald or had the motive, if nothing else. And she's obviously convinced the affair happened."

"She's shown a violent streak as well. Maybe she's protesting his guilt so loudly because she's deflecting attention away from herself," Teagan offered.

"Wouldn't Ella have been her target?" George thought Natalia might be capable of it, but what would her motivation have been? Ronald, if anything, was an equally wounded party.

"Maybe Ella was the target. The drink could've gone to the wrong person, and now she's trying to cover her tracks." Teagan made an excellent point. George hadn't considered Ronald not being the original target. "I'd say put an asterisk next to their names on your list."

"So, what did Natalia say when you popped into her shop?" Murphy asked the question George had politely been avoiding. He hadn't wanted to press but was desperately curious. "Did she say anything about Darren?"

"She called him an absolute wanker about twenty times in the space of a minute." Teagan moved away from Margo and returned to the armchair they'd claimed. "I honestly didn't get much out of her. On the other hand, though, she did mutter something about not letting Ella drag them down with her."

"Intriguing." Margo finished pouring tea for everyone and set the pot aside. She grabbed her cup and went to sit in the chair beside Teagan's. "Maybe she thinks Ella did it."

"Maybe she thinks they both did it." George grabbed the notebook Margo had left on the coffee table. "Trying to get rid of the husband so they can be together?"

"Maybe she's worried she's next?" Murphy stretched his arm across the back of the sofa. His hand rested on George's shoulder, giving it a light squeeze. "I'm wondering if we should tell Sarah."

"That we eavesdropped on a domestic, then theorised the husband may or may not be plotting to kill the wife?" George didn't think they had anything concrete at all. "I've watched enough telly to know the police will think we have vivid imaginations."

"We do. Well, you do. Remember those stories you used to write?" Margo teased him with a good-natured grin.

"It's not my fault. Ma told me to write down my dreams. So I did. How am I to blame for how ridiculously vivid they were?" George had suffered night terrors as a child and teenager. His parents had suggested journaling as a way to get the thoughts out of his head. It hadn't helped, but the stories had been creative. "All I'm saying is if we tell Sarah now, she'll think we're gossiping. And it doesn't look brilliant when they've already dragged Murphy in for questioning."

"And I am not anxious for a repeat." Murphy grabbed his phone out of his pocket when it buzzed. "Sarah heard about the argument."

"I imagine everyone in the entire village has heard about the Fishwicks going at it in the middle of the street by now." George had no doubts the story had spread like a virus. Nothing stayed secret in a little place like Dufftown. "Everyone's already in everyone's business here. A couple shouting and throwing vases? I imagine half of Cornwall knows about it by now."

"He's not wrong," Margo readily concurred. "The WhatsApp group chat for the local paramedics was buzzing about it before you'd even gotten to my door. Everyone wanted all the details about Darren's dust-up with his wife. He's not the most well-liked bloke. Tends to rub people the wrong way."

"He rubbed Ella—"

"Teagan." Murphy cut them off before they could finish.

"All I'm saying is he rubbed at least one person the right way." Teagan snickered before hiding behind their cup of tea. "Sorry."

"How do we figure out if Darren was actually involved?" George decided to bring the conversation back around to a more comfortable topic.

"We could always ask him." Murphy adjusted his arm around George, ignoring the looks from Teagan and Margo. "Maybe it's time for a little subtle prodding."

ELEVEN

MURPHY

"You could ask Margo out." Murphy threw the question at Teagan while they were driving him home. "I'm pretty sure she'd say yes."

"I'm aware. She already said yes." Teagan grinned when he cheered them on and gave their arm a light punch. "I didn't want to wait until we were as old and grey as you."

"Rude. But also, she said yes?" Murphy teased. He was happy for his younger friend. They'd had a crush on Margo for a while. He frowned when he noticed the caution tape still littering the ground near the brewery. "Who do you think did it?"

"Bertrand."

"No hesitation at all? Why?"

"Motive. How often do you hear on true crime docs about how they followed the money to the killer? It's a devil of a thing." Teagan parked in their usual spot. They tapped their fingers against the steering wheel. "People do funny shite when they're afraid of losing access to their cash."

"I doubt we can count on Bertrand getting into a row in the middle of the street."

"You let me worry about Bertrand. His girlfriend pops into my auntie's hair salon all the time." Teagan ran their fingers along the side of their hair. "My dye job could use a touch-up. Maybe I'll find myself there the next time she is."

"Simple as that?"

"You'd be amazed at what people natter about when getting their hair done." Teagan shooed him out of their vehicle. "Are we open for business tomorrow?"

"Think I'll take the day. The police don't want the pub open. It's not been that long. We're not going to be ruined if we're shut for a week." Murphy got out of the car. He crouched down to grab a stray bit of the police caution tape. "I'll probably spend the time cleaning up the mess the forensic team left. Sanitise the place."

"Why don't you let us give you a hand? I'm sure Maisie and Graeme wouldn't mind either. It's why you employ us, after all." Teagan made him promise to give his brother and sister-in-law a call. "I'll chat with you later."

Once Teagan had driven off, Murphy decided to step into the pub. He hadn't gone inside since the police had taken him in for questioning. The mess wasn't as bad as he'd anticipated.

There was fingerprint powder dusted over multiple surfaces. Glasses were still strewn about; some had been knocked over, with sticky mead remnants on the floor or the bar counter. It wasn't going to be easy to clean up the liquid.

"Well, shite." Murphy rubbed the back of his neck for a moment. He balled up the caution tape in his hand and took stock of everything. "Maybe I should call in reinforcements."

Grabbing the large rubbish bin from the kitchen, Murphy dragged it out into the pub. He tossed the caution tape into it and began clearing up the trash. He'd deal with the glasses next.

He'd just finished with the first phase of his plan when the pub door opened. Graeme gave a low whistle when he got a good look at the state of the pub. He rolled up his sleeves and came over to join his brother.

"Maisie's visiting her mum, so when Teagan called, I thought I'd give you a hand." Graeme began gathering up some of the glasses off the floor. "What's with all the dust?"

"Fingerprints, I assume."

"Ah." Graeme carried a load of glasses into the kitchen and returned with one of their large serving trays. "Why didn't you call?"

"I thought I'd make a head start."

"Stubborn bastard." Graeme shook his head. He began stacking glasses onto the tray, carefully balancing them on the counter. "You don't have to sort everything out on your own, Paddy. Just because you're the eldest."

"I wasn't trying to do it all." Murphy finished dumping another stack of rubbish in the bin. He'd picked up all the larger bits already, so he grabbed the broom and began sweeping. "This helps me organise my thoughts. The last few days have been absolutely mental. I'm trying to sort through the chaos."

"Fair enough. You're still a grumpy, stubborn bastard."

"Yeah, but I've been like that since I came out of

the womb." Murphy smirked before dodging the crumpled napkin thrown in his direction. He frowned when he noticed ink on it. "What's this?"

Carefully unravelling the napkin, Murphy squinted at the smudged words. He moved closer to one of the lamps on the wall for better lighting. It didn't help.

Flattening the napkin out a little more, Murphy managed to make out half of the sentence. *Do it now.* The writing was too smudged for him to identify the penmanship or figure out the whole meaning. It was an extraordinary thing to find after a murder, though.

Murphy didn't think it was a coincidence. "Where was this?"

"Squashed under the bar."

"Where specifically?" Murphy came around to see where Graeme was pointing. Under the bar counter, there was a small gap. It was perfect for a squashed napkin. "Why here?"

"The bowls of dry ice were set up right above it." Graeme gestured to the counter above the gap. "I only noticed because I'd bent down to pick up a glass right in front of it. Never would've seen otherwise. They'd shoved it all the way inside."

"Maybe they were running out of time? Someone came up to them. Maisie was back and forth the whole night. She might've been heading towards the killer without even knowing it." Murphy set the napkin down on the counter. He took a photo with his phone before texting his cousin. "I'll let Sarah know what we found. The last thing I need is the police assuming I'm hiding something."

"Text Evan as well. He'll want to be updated on any interaction with the police." Graeme had an excellent point. He nodded towards the camera behind them. "Good news is the security footage will show how and where I found it, so they can't accuse us of anything."

By the time Murphy finished his message to his solicitor, Sarah had responded to his text. She told him to leave the napkin on the counter. One of the detectives would swing by to pick it up along with the camera footage. Of course, they'd also want Graeme's statement regarding it.

"Brilliant. Bang goes my day." Graeme sighed. "Well, they do say no good deed goes unpunished. Last time I offer to help you clean up."

"Don't I pay you for this shite?" Murphy snickered at his younger brother.

Teasing each other a little more, they returned to cleaning up the pub. They'd made good progress on getting all of the glasses into the kitchen and sweeping up by the time Detective Constable Smith arrived. He placed the napkin into an evidence bag, took the disc with the security footage, and got a brief statement from Graeme.

"Could you both try to keep out of the investigation? Please? For my sake and Sarah's?" Elwin Smith had grown up with them. He'd been in the same class as Graeme at school. "I'd prefer not to interrogate either of you about something I know you didn't do."

"We didn't plan to find a napkin, Elrond." Graeme grinned when his old schoolmate glowered at him.

"I am *not* an elf."

"You've got the ears." Graeme held his hands up in surrender. "Sorry. I'm not trying to be difficult."

"You've never had to try." Elwin closed his notebook and shoved it into his pocket. "Just stay out of the investigation. Don't think I didn't hear about you lot being bang in the middle of the dust-up between the Fishwicks earlier."

"With those ears? Bet you hear loads." Graeme darted away when Elwin started towards him. "Oi. Police intimidation."

"If you two could act for all of a minute that you aren't in primary school, I would greatly appreciate it," Murphy interrupted after watching the two old friends pretend to swat at each other. "Can you tell us anything about the investigation?"

"Not officially."

"Unofficially?" Graeme leaned against the counter. "C'mon, Elwin. Give us a hint of something, or I'll tell your mum what really happened to her favourite garden gnome."

"You absolute bastard." Elwin was, for the briefest second, more of a stroppy teenager than a detective constable. He finally gave a shrug and answered them. "We're looking into his wife. And after the domestic in the village, we're also going to be questioning the Fishwicks, since they both attended your mead tasting."

"We know that," Graeme complained.

"You should've been more specific. I best get this napkin to forensics for testing. Try not to stumble on any other scraps of paper or bodies, will you?" Elwin headed out of the pub, waving the evidence bag at them. "And don't leave the country."

"I remember when you two...."

"Nope. Not going down an embarrassing memory lane with you." Graeme cut him off before he could even start. "I'm going to get this last tray of glasses into the dishwasher, then I'm afraid I'm going to have to jog on, or I'll be late to pick Maisie up."

Ten minutes later, Murphy found himself alone in the pub. They'd gathered all of the glasses and other dishes. He'd swept the floor and picked up all the rubbish.

Once Murphy had dealt with the rubbish bags, he turned his attention to mopping the floor. He'd grabbed a disinfectant. Unfortunately, his gaze kept drifting to the spot where Ronald had died.

Was anyone ever going to be able to step foot in the pub without thinking about a man dying there?

After mopping for the seventh time, Murphy decided he'd done all he possibly could to sanitise the area. First, he made sure everything was dry, then switched to the cleaner specifically for wooden floors. It would keep him from ruining the finish if he hadn't already.

For the briefest second, Murphy considered putting a sign on the spot. *Here died Ronald.* It was macabre and probably in bad taste. On the other hand, he didn't know if he should simply ignore it.

A problem for another day.

They wouldn't be able to open the pub for a few days. He didn't know if the police would want to come back since they'd missed the napkin. And he wasn't ready to play host to a bar full of curious villagers who'd all have questions.

Murphy left the pub, locking up behind him. He wanted to check on things in his office before heading upstairs to his little flat above the brewery. He paused when he noticed an unfamiliar car parked beside his. A man stepped out and started towards him. "Can I help you?"

"You sent someone to bother my girlfriend."

"Excuse me?" Murphy frowned. It took him a second to place where he knew the man from. "Bertrand Donelson. You're Ronald's brother."

"You *sent* someone to bother my girlfriend." Bertrand was a little taller than his brother had been. He had an inch or two on Murphy and attempted to loom menacingly over him. "The bloody hell are you on about?"

"I haven't sent anyone to do anything." Murphy hadn't exactly lied. He didn't ask Teagan to hang around her auntie's place. "Think you've got the wrong end of the stick."

Bertrand lunged forward. He grabbed Murphy by his shirt and tried to shove him into the wall behind him. "I didn't kill my sodding brother."

"I haven't accused you of anything." Murphy caught Bertrand by the wrists and pried his hands off his shirt. He shoved the man away from him. "You may be taller, but I've a feeling I'm a good deal stronger. You've seen me at the Highland Games every year. Calm yourself down. What are you talking about?"

"I don't know." Bertrand shook his head. He seemed to finally calm himself down enough to think more clearly. "Your..."

"Careful." Murphy rarely lost his temper, but he'd brook no insult to Teagan or anyone he cared about.

"Teagan. Works with you here? My girl goes to her aunt's place. She said they were all poking and prodding around about Ronnie's murder. They kept asking about the money." Bertrand clenched his fists at his side. He started forward only to stop when he caught the look in Murphy's eye. "You're trying to throw suspicion off yourself. Police dragged you off the night of the murder. Bet you're just looking to say I did it."

"If not you, then who wanted your brother dead?"

"Despite what the rumour mill thinks, I control my own sodding inheritance. My brother was a self-righteous twit, but I wasn't going to off him for money." Bertrand appeared to be expending a great deal of effort into controlling his temper. "His wife's a cold fish. Not even in the grave, and she's already emptied the house of his things. I drove by to find all of it being loaded into the back of a lorry."

Well, shite.

TWELVE

GEORGE

"GRIEF AFFECTS EVERYONE DIFFERENTLY, BUT it's a wee bit soon to be throwing out all his effects." George had come over with Bumble not long after Bertrand had finally taken off. He'd brought over a mutton curry shepherd's pie, a combination of two family recipes. They'd taken it up to Murphy's flat above the brewery. "She tossed all of it?"

"On a lorry for a trip to the tip."

"Think we could get a look at it? Maybe there's a reason she wanted it out of the house so quickly." George found it incredibly suspicious. "I wonder if the police know she's potentially gotten rid of some evidence."

"Exactly how much true crime are you watching when you can't sleep?" Murphy took a bite of the shepherd's pie. "More delicious than the last time. What's the secret?"

"Ancient family secrets. A little Indian, a little Scottish. All blended together in my favourite dish." George had taken recipes from his grand-mothers on both sides and combined them. He waved his fork around, sending mashed potato flying. "You know everyone in the village. What about someone who might get us access to Ronald's rubbish?"

"I don't know everyone, but I might have someone I can call." Murphy sighed when George smirked at him. "Sarah's going to kill both of us."

"Aren't the police supposed to avoid killing inno-cent civilians?" George finished up his meal. He set the plate to the side and pulled out the notebook Margo had given him. "Are we crossing Bertrand off the list of suspects?"

"Darren and Natalia are our only proof that Ronald controlled his inheritance." Murphy pointed out. "What if they were speaking at the crime scene on purpose? Hoping the police or someone else would overhear?"

"A misdirection? 'We certainly didn't kill anyone, so let's talk loudly about someone who had a motive at the crime scene.'" George thought about what they'd witnessed outside of the coffee shop. "What if the entire argument was staged?"

"Natalia's not a good enough actress to pull it off —and she's always had a temper." Murphy finished his last bite of food. He set his plate on top of George's, carrying both across the room to his kitchenette. "You've a fair point. They made a spectacle of themselves in a place they'd be certain of an audience."

"Both times." George found it hard to believe people would put so much effort into building a lie. "Could they really be capable of such duplicity?"

"To set up a smokescreen for a murder? People have done weirder things to avoid justice." Murphy began washing up the plates. He put the leftovers into his fridge, much to George's amusement. "I suppose the question is how do we prove anything at all?"

"We don't. The police do."

"Weren't you the one who wanted to solve this?"

"Solve? Yes. Prove? Not sure we can do that." George flipped through the pages of his notebook. He glanced over at Bumble, who pawed to get down. Once on the floor, he immediately made his way over to the little bed Murphy had set up in the corner by the window. "We need to talk to Ella."

"She is *not* going to talk to me. Not when she's swearing up and down I killed her husband." Murphy finished up with the dishes. He dried his hands off and tossed the towel to one side. "Might see if Teagan or Margo has any ideas. It can't be either of us. We're going to trigger a reaction."

"Maybe we want to trigger a reaction from her. If she killed her husband or knows who did, it might be the only way to see the truth." George jotted down what they'd learned from Bertrand and what they suspected. "He could be lying."

"They could all be lying."

"Wouldn't an inheritance like the Donelsons' have required a solicitor? Maybe Evan's heard something." George knew because of attorney-client privilege the actual person who handled the will and trusts would never speak to them. "I doubt he represented them, so maybe he's heard rumours."

"Attorney-client privilege."

"On rumours about a client that's not his?" George wasn't surprised when Murphy went for his phone. "They might not disclose details with each other, but they're human beings underneath the legal façade. In my experience, people will talk."

While Murphy had a quick conversation with their solicitor friend, George flipped to a new section in his notebook. He jotted down what they knew about each suspect. Ella and Bertrand went on the same page.

Had the bitter wife who wanted to leave her husband without losing money done it? Or had Bertrand lied to Murphy? Was Roland in control of his inheritance after all?

Then, there were the wild cards—Darren and Natalia. The former had a clear motive against Ronald. The latter would surely have been angrier with her own husband or Ella.

"If Natalia was involved, why would she have wanted to kill Ronald? He was as much of a victim in the affair as she was," George muttered to himself and Bumble, who snuffled and went back to sleep. He turned his question to Murphy once he'd gotten off the phone. "What do you think?"

"About?"

"Why would Natalia kill Ronald instead of Darren or Ella? What's the motive?" George absently doodled on the margin of the page. "It doesn't make sense."

"So, either she's not involved."

"Possible. Or, she's protecting her husband."

"Or she meant for the drink to go to Darren or Ella." George knew his thoughts were going around in circles. "Maybe they really were having a real massive row in the middle of the village?"

"Maybe. If it smells like a duck...."

"How do you know what a duck smells like?" George rubbed his eyes tiredly for a moment. "Do you go around grabbing them and sniffing them?"

"No." Murphy gave a choked noise.

"Good to know. What did Evan say?" George didn't have the energy to decipher neurotypical reactions.

Murphy stared at him for a few seconds before finally responding. "He said we should keep our noses out of a police inquiry."

George rolled his eyes. He had no doubts Evan was as curious as they were about who'd killed Ronald. "What did he say when he was finished being sensible for the sake of legal liability?"

"He has no direct knowledge about the Donelson will or inheritance. But he does recall being in close proximity when Bertrand and Ronald had an altercation outside of their solicitor's office. The younger brother was going on a tear about being screwed out of control over his own life." Murphy came over to sit beside him. He leaned in closer, throwing a heavy arm casually over George's shoulders. "Ol' Bertie either lied to my face, or things changed at some point."

"Like after he murdered his brother?" George absolutely did not snuggle into Murphy's side. It just looked like he had.

Bumble eyed them from the floor before snuffling back to sleep. George exchanged a grin with Murphy when the snoring picked up again. It was never completely quiet in a house with a pug.

The silence between them dragged on for a few minutes. George enjoyed it. He jotted down a few thoughts in the notebook while resting against Murphy.

Murphy tapped his finger against a note about Bertrand. "Still curious about why he tracked me down?"

"Maybe he was protecting his girlfriend? Have you asked Teagan for their side of the conversation?" George knew them well enough to know they could manage a subtle conversation if required. "Tell them to bring pain au chocolat from the bakery. I want something sweet."

"Too late for the bakery. Doesn't she close up shop at six?"

"Bugger." George had been craving chocolate all day. "Fine, fine. No chocolate for me."

"I'm sure Teagan can find chocolate for you. Should we invite Margo?"

"Margo doesn't like driving." George knew his cousin would also be irritated at missing out on yet another "let's pretend we're detectives" session. "And I am vastly understating her feelings on the subject."

"Maybe Teagan can pick her up." Murphy snickered.

"Why is that funny?"

"My Teagan has a crush on your cousin."

"Still not seeing the joke. You're being decidedly neurotypical." George froze. He held a hand up to stop Murphy from responding to him. "Did you hear that?"

"Hear what?"

"Shh." George strained to hear. He moved towards the door leading down to the brewery, opening it and standing at the top of the stairs. "I swear I heard—"

Despite the darkness in the brewery, George crept down the stairs. He'd definitely heard something coming from either outside or downstairs. It was difficult to tell.

Pausing halfway down the stairs, George listened carefully. He heard Murphy behind him and

Bumble's nails on the wooden floor. It was almost impossible for him to tune them out.

With a sigh of frustration, George continued down the stairs. He'd gotten to the bottom when he heard glass breaking outside. *Shite.* He rushed towards the door, slamming into a table in the process.

"Bugger."

"Maybe turn on a light?"

"They'll see us." George had no idea who he was talking about. But someone or something had shattered glass outside. "Maybe we should try sneaking up on them? We might catch them before they run off."

Deciding they were wasting too much time, George crept through the brewery. He was a little more careful moving through the darkened room until he safely reached the door. Murphy had caught up to him; he had Bumble in his arms, obviously having picked him up on the journey down the stairs.

George paused with his hand on the doorknob when he heard more glass breaking. "You heard that? Right? I'm not imagining things."

"You're definitely not imagining things. Why don't you take Bumble? I'll..."

"Why? Because you're bigger?" George huffed. "There's power in numbers. You protect Bumble."

They tried to open the door as quietly as possible. At the last second, Murphy reached over to switch the outside lights on. The parking area was suddenly bathed in light.

George got the briefest glimpse of someone dressed in black before they bolted down the lane. "Oi."

"George." Murphy tried to grab him but missed his arm.

Racing after the person, George had a second to notice the broken windows on both of their vehicles. He picked up speed, trying to catch up with their vandal. They somehow managed to pick up more speed, moving out of view around a corner.

George skidded to a halt at the end of the lane. He couldn't see anyone running in either direction. It took him a few seconds to catch his breath. "Coward."

Murphy met him halfway back down the lane. He was struggling to contain Bumble in his arms. He had his phone in his other hand. "Have you lost your mind?"

"No, it seems to still be intact. I lost sight of them." George rescued Bumble from his grasp, pulling a lead from his pocket and attaching it to his collar before setting him down on the ground. "Did you call the police?"

"They broke windows in both of our vehicles. And I can see where they tried to force their way into the pub." Murphy crouched down when they were back at the brewery and picked Bumble up. "I don't want him to risk his little paws getting cut on glass. Make sure not to touch anything."

"Our fingerprints are already going to be on our vehicles." George shoved his hands into his pockets to avoid the temptation.

"Not on whatever they used to break all the windows." Murphy handed Bumble to George. He disappeared into the brewery and then returned with a torch that he shone into the vehicle. "Looks like a stone. Probably picked it up from the broken wall behind the pub."

"Crime of opportunity? Maybe lost their temper when they couldn't get into the brewery?" George absently petted Bumble, who panted contentedly in his arms. "Why would they try to get into the pub?"

"Maybe they were looking for the napkin."

"*Shite.*" George hadn't thought about that. "Maybe they figured they could come back to grab it after the police were finished?"

"And I wouldn't notice?"

"If it is the killer? Maybe they're so desperate to get rid of the evidence that it was worth the risk?" George stepped over to peer into the back of his vehicle. It seemed like the vandal had simply thrown rocks without any purpose. Nothing was missing from his Range Rover. "It was dark out, but maybe your security cameras caught them?"

"They had their face covered, from the glimpse I got."

"It wasn't Natalia." George knew that for absolute certainty. "The person was too tall and lithe to be her. She couldn't hide her curves under a hoodie."

Murphy waved him towards the brewery. "Why don't we wait inside? I want to check the CCTV system. Maybe they got a better look at them than we did."

"I had a fantastic view of the back of their hoodie." George rested his head against Bumble, rubbing his face against his fur. "Why risk it? They had to have seen our vehicles."

"What would you risk if there was one piece of evidence to prove your guilt in a murder?"

"I wouldn't risk anything by committing the crime in the first place." George set Bumble down in Murphy's office. He watched the pug stretch briefly before waddling over to collapse into the bed next to the desk. "How many beds are you going to buy for him?"

"As many as he needs. And I was speaking metaphorically, not literally."

"I suppose I'd do anything."

"Exactly." Murphy twisted his laptop around so they could watch while he pulled up the security cameras. "They just didn't know I'd already turned the napkin over to the police."

THIRTEEN

MURPHY

THE SECURITY CAMERAS HAD PICKED UP EVERY detail of the attempted theft and the vandalism except the suspect's face. They gave Constable Davie the footage. He called out the detectives to inspect the broken glass as well.

Sarah had not been thrilled at George giving chase of the suspect. He just stared at Bumble and ignored her lecture. Murphy tried not to laugh.

While George often struggled with a lot of social things at times, he'd turned pretending to listen to someone into an art. The only thing that gave him away was occasionally nodding in the wrong spots. Bumble made it easier by being adorably distracting.

Teagan arrived in the middle of the chaos.

They'd brought along a box of pastries from their auntie. Murphy teased his cousin about getting sugar in her precious notebook; Sarah responded by threatening to arrest him.

"It's late. I'm going to suggest you all go home and get some rest. And for the love of god, leave us to do the investigating. I'm begging you." Sarah finished taking notes and motioned for the constable. "Paddy."

"I hear you." Murphy had no intentions of listening to her. Curiosity had sunk its teeth into him. He wanted to know what had happened in his pub that almost led to him being arrested for murder. "Don't stay up too late. You look like you need more beauty rest."

"You're such an arsehole." Sarah glowered at her cousin before finally stowing away her little notebook. "Just... try not to get yourselves killed or involved in another murder inquiry, will you?"

"We'll do our best," Murphy promised.

They stood outside, watching the police leave. Once they were gone, Murphy grabbed a few large bin liners and duct tape. He sealed the broken windows as best he could; they'd definitely have to call the auto shop to get them fixed in the morning.

"Why don't we get some tea? We can have pastries, and I'll tell you everything I learned at my auntie's salon." Teagan tapped the box in their arms. "I've got all the tea."

"Okay. But you are Tea?" George carried Bumble into the brewery with him. They all went up the stairs into Murphy's flat. "Tea spilling tea?"

"You're not allowed on YouTube again." Teagan set the box on the kitchen counter, opened the lid, and selected one of the delectable treats for themselves. "Ol' Bertie's girlfriend is an interesting piece of work. She was more than happy to tell everyone all about his older brother."

"Yeah?" Murphy went over to fill his electric kettle. He pulled down several mismatched mugs. "I've got the three-in-one tea packets your auntie brought back on her last trip."

"Instant masala? Brilliant."

"You would like sugary milk tea." Teagan didn't complain when Murphy mixed up a mug for them as well. "So, this bint basically claimed Ronald held the purse strings tightly. He once cut Bertrand off for failing one of his university courses."

"Interesting." George had made sure Bumble was snug in his little bed before grabbing a sugar-dusted, jam-filled pastry for himself. "I imagine that might've put a strain on their relationship."

"She also said Bertrand and Roland had a massive row a few weeks ago." Teagan paused to take a large bite of their pastry. "Apparently, the elder brother turned down the younger by refusing to allow him to take a chunk out of his trust to start his own business."

"Sounds like a power struggle." Murphy finished up with the tea. He carried the three mugs over, setting them down on the coffee table before taking a seat beside George. "Why would Bertrand lie to me about it? I have no impact on the case aside from being brought in for questioning."

"Maybe he thought you'd share it with Sarah or one of the other detectives?" George sank back into the cushions with the mug in his hands. "Are we certain he wasn't at the tasting?"

"Didn't see him on any of the security footage." Murphy had gone back through every single second of it. He hadn't seen the younger Donelson brother at all. "Someone obviously was. Someone left a note saying, 'do it now.' Maybe he had more than one accomplice?"

"Hmm." George hummed. He sipped the milky tea with a contented sigh. "I wonder what was in the rubbish Ella tossed out. She was in such a hurry to throw away her husband's things. Right after his murder. It's suspicious."

"Is there something beyond suspicious? Because it feels more than that." Teagan grabbed a cushion off the couch and sat on the floor beside Bumble. "Aren't you just the bestest dog in the whole world? You definitely are."

"Let me text one of Graeme's old schoolmates. He works at the Keith recycling centre. I'm betting they took the stuff there. If we're lucky, they haven't gotten rid of all of it." Murphy had a feeling it was probably too late, but maybe something in the rubbish had stood out. Anything was better than nothing. "Did you hear anything else while adding more colour to your hair?"

Teagan patted the side of their head where the colours had been noticeably brightened. "Not from the girlfriend. My auntie mentioned Ronald Donelson had been seen at a solicitor's office in Keith."

"Not that much of a surprise."

"A family law solicitor," Teagan added. "Reeve and Foster? I think. Don't they mostly handle divorce and custody situations?"

"Ah. Interesting. Old money like the Donelson's?

I bet you there was a prenup. But, of course, they'd want to protect their precious history." Murphy finished his message to Graeme's friend and opened the thread to Evan. He'd been licking his wounds a little after Margo had turned him down. "Anyone have plans for tomorrow?"

"Not working since we're shut for the next few days." Teagan stretched their legs out, still sipping on their tea. "Why?"

"I'm going to take a trip out to the recycling centre, then swing by Keith to have a chat with Evan about divorce, prenups, and trust funds." Murphy figured it would keep him from stressing at home in his flat. Unfortunately, his tendency to hermit wasn't going to serve him well, with a murder still looming over him. "Anyone want to join me?"

"I will. Might let Bumble enjoy a playdate with Treacle." George had his own phone out, likely messaging Margo to see if she was free.

"Only your dog would have a playdate." Teagan grinned. They laughed when Bumble let out a loud snort. "My apologies. I shouldn't have poked fun at you for spending time with your bestie."

"He takes his Treacle time very seriously." George dropped his phone onto the couch beside him. "Besides, he'll have more fun there than traipsing through the rubbish with us."

"Not sure how much traipsing will happen." Murphy reached out to take George's hand. He rubbed his thumb across his knuckles. "Make sure to wear your wellies."

"You're both disgustingly adorable. I might be violently ill."

FOURTEEN

GEORGE

IT HAD BEEN ANOTHER LONG NIGHT WITH NOT A lot of sleep. George struggled to get his mind to shut down. He woke up with a mild headache and Bumble drooling on his chest.

The alarm on his phone had been going off for a good twenty minutes. He had it set to a pleasing classical piece. It normally woke him up if Bumble hadn't trampled all over his face.

"C'mon. Time for us to get up and going. You've got your best friend waiting for you. But first, breakfast and bees." George dragged a T-shirt over his head and padded barefoot into the bathroom. He splashed icy-cold water on his face until he felt a little less like absolute shite. "Nothing like murder to ruin my peaceful night of sleep."

Making his way into the kitchen, George immediately turned the kettle on for coffee. He stared blearily at the calendar on the fridge. It was where he kept his bee schedule and a list of daily to-dos.

The ones that never changed. His mind often remembered the odd tasks out, but the daily ones slipped past him. The list on the calendar ensured he didn't miss any critical stages with his bees. It was particularly important in the summer when he had to concentrate on collecting nectar.

Much of his time was spent ensuring the health of the hive. He checked daily for any issues with his colony. It was imperative to keep an eye out for disease or swarming.

He'd almost lost his entire colony of bees because of a critical mistake early on his beekeeping. It had made him hypervigilant as a result, hence the calendar. He breathed a little easier after checking on them and ensuring they were buzzing along merrily around the hives.

"Ready for your playdate?" George had managed a quick shower and breakfast. Bumble had eyed him suspiciously, since he wasn't a fan of baths. "Don't worry; I'm not going to attempt to drown you today. As your auntie Margo would say, you're such a drama queen."

Whizzing around the garden to quickly check on everything, George made it out the door with Bumble a few minutes later than expected. He didn't have time to stress about seeing Murphy. Not that he usually was anxious, but they were slowly dancing their way into a relationship; it somehow felt like it mattered more.

Margo was, as per usual, waiting at the door for him. Treacle lazed on the grass in front of the cottage. George had to carefully extract a struggling Bumble, who wanted down immediately.

The two cousins watched their dogs for a moment in silence. They were the sweetest of best friends. Bumble didn't take long to find the perfect spot in the garden to lounge on with Treacle draped across him.

"So, tell me about Teagan." George was running late, but he always had a little time to tease Margo. "Murphy said Evan had asked you out."

"Evan and I are friends. Nothing more. Teagan asked me in on a date."

"In on a date?" George found himself intrigued by the idea.

"They won't tell me what they're planning, just that I won't have to go anywhere." Margo shrugged. "Leave them alone. No pressing them for answers."

"Yeah, yeah." George gave Margo a quick hug, then petted both Treacle and Bumble. Both dogs were unmoved by him. They were more interested in watching a passing bumblebee. "I see where I rate."

Murphy texted him halfway to the brewery, suggesting he drive straight to the auto shop. Lenny had promised to fix the windows on both of their vehicles while lending them one of his spare cars for a few days. It depended on how long it took him to get the glass in.

When George arrived at Lenny's shop, Murphy was already waiting outside for him. They walked a few streets over to grab coffee and stopped by Evan's office. He didn't have any concrete information to share, so they returned to the shop and grabbed Lenny's keys.

"Oi. Got a second?" Lenny whistled sharply, drawing their attention. He rubbed his oil-covered hands on a rag. "Heard you were heading out to the recycling centre."

"Yeah? When'd you talk to Maisie?"

"She called my missus at eight last night to have a natter about something." Lenny was married to Maisie's cousin. "Anyway, spoke to my mate who runs the centre about what you're searching for."

"Oh?"

"Turns out they're behind by a few days. Some machine broke. Since the toff tossed the stuff, it's free and available for anyone who wants to poke their nose into it. Just tell Seamus at the gate that I sent you." Lenny waved them off with his oily rag. "Off with you. I've got work to do. Don't fall in any waste compactors. And I want an invitation to the wedding."

"Shut up, greasy bastard."

"Oil, not grease," Lenny retorted.

George snickered at Murphy and Lenny, who exchanged a few more insults before they finally drove away. "I can never tell if you're friends or not."

"In school, Lenny and I were more often than not on the same side of arguments. He's a good bloke. I enjoy needling him." Murphy guided the car down the lane towards the recycling centre. "We don't mean anything by it."

George didn't always understand the nuances of neurotypical friendships. He tried his best but often found himself making a fool of himself. It was why he kept his circle small. "Do you think we're going to find anything?"

"Define anything? We may find old clothes and books. We might find the metaphorical smoking gun." Murphy shrugged. He reached down to rest his hand on George's leg. "I've no idea. Still not certain why the police haven't searched through it."

"Should we be touching any of it?"

"I brought gloves from the brewery. We can keep our fingerprints off anything so Sarah won't scream at us too much. Pretty sure I'm getting coal in my stocking, whatever happens." Murphy left his hand on George's leg as if it were completely natural. "Not exactly how I hoped to spend our second date."

"Rummaging through someone else's rubbish?"

They found Seamus easily enough. Tall, ginger, and smoking a pipe. If being Scottish was a super-power, the man definitely had it in spades. All he needed was a kilt. He motioned them to an empty parking space and led them into the building once they'd gotten out of the car.

George leaned into Murphy while they walked behind Seamus. "Am I the only one who keeps hearing bagpipes?"

"Aye. That's my theme music." Seamus winked at them. "Here's all her stuff. I'd planned to go through it today and send some of it to my ma's charity shop."

There were several stacked boxes, along with a few large bags. Murphy pulled out the gloves from his pocket and handed a pair to George. Seamus raised his bushy eyebrows but walked away without comment.

"Super Scot. He's fuelled by haggis." Murphy grinned at George. "I take part in the Highland Games every year and I'm not as Scottish as he is."

With a snicker, George grabbed the bag closest to him. It was jam-packed with clothes. There was everything from boxers to several expensive suits. Had she literally thrown away every single article of clothing in his closet?

"Why didn't she send these to a charity shop? Aren't toffs like her always going on about doing more for the less fortunate? 'One does what one can, doesn't one?'" George mimicked her mannerism almost perfectly. He held up a winter coat. "This has to be worth a few hundred quid."

"Odd that she'd simply chuck everything away within days of his death. I know people grieve in different ways, but even so." Murphy lifted a dark grey suit with a double-breasted jacket out of a bag. "William Hunt. This is tailored. I bet this was easily a thousand quid."

"And she threw it out?" George shook his head in surprise. "Why? It's such a waste. We should check all the pockets. Never know what we might find."

Going through the pockets of all the clothing in

the four bags took forever. They hadn't even opened any of the boxes yet. They had a small stack of papers and a few candy wrappers when they finished.

"This is interesting." George held out a scrap of paper with a date and name. "Isn't this the family law solicitor? The one Evan believed worked with the Donelsons?"

"It is. So a week before his death, Ronald was seeing his solicitor. Was it for a divorce or something to do with his brother's money? I doubt they'll tell us anything. Let me take a photo. We're definitely going to have to let Sarah know." Murphy sighed. He inspected another folded note from another pocket. "This one's from an estate agent."

"An estate agent? How interesting." George flipped through the rest of the papers that he'd gathered up. "Nothing else of interest. Most of this is receipts or business cards. Nothing incriminating. He had an unhealthy obsession with sweets. I can't believe the number of wrappers I've found in his pockets. Was he a little old man disguised as someone in their thirties?"

"No idea." Murphy used his phone to get photos of the two papers they'd found. "Sending this to

Elwin instead of Sarah. He's less likely to get aggravated."

"You mean, less likely to tell you he's aggravated with you." George moved over to one of the boxes. He pulled the flaps apart and stared in stunned amazement. "Books. Some of these are very old and probably worth some money. Why throw them out?"

"Spite? If he cared about them, maybe she's snubbing her nose at him by throwing out prized possessions or family heirlooms?" Murphy stepped up beside him. He picked up one of the books, flipping through it to see it was over a hundred years old. "We're going to have to be careful with these. I wouldn't want to damage them. Seamus might be able to donate them to a library or sell them."

"If you had a cheating wife with no value for books, where would you hide your secrets?" George gingerly flipped through the first novel he'd picked up. "This could be a complete waste of time."

"I'm with you; combing through books to look for a clue to point to a murder doesn't seem like a waste of time to me. Sounds like a brilliant way to spend my day." Murphy set the book in his hand down and reached for another one. "The collected works of Shakespeare. Think they ever read these?"

"Only if to appear impressive to all their friends

and probably at boarding school." George grabbed a random history book. He carefully went through all the pages and found nothing before picking up another one. "Oh, hello, what are you?"

"Find something?"

"An envelope." George extracted it from the middle of the book. There was no writing on the outside to identify where it was from or who it had been sent to. "Should we open it?"

Before Murphy could respond, his phone gave a jaunty ring. He answered immediately. George listened while Detective Constable Elwin Smith lectured; he was so loud it was easy to hear both sides of the conversation.

George ran his finger underneath the envelope flap. "I suppose we shouldn't open this."

Murphy slid his phone back into his pocket. "Elwin's on his way. He wants to collect the evidence himself. He said not to touch anything we haven't already looked at."

"I've already touched this." George waved the envelope in his hand. His curiosity was definitely getting the better of him. What was inside? A love letter? A will? Didn't detectives always find something of that sort in the best murder mysteries? "I'm dying to know what it is."

"Could be nothing." Murphy moved around the box to stand next to him. "Or, it could be something."

"Are you always this profound after an hour of digging around in rubbish?" George teased. He pushed open the envelope flap. "Oh look, it's open. I guess we'll have to see what's inside."

With a snort of amusement, Murphy reached out to take the envelope's contents. It was several sheets of folded paper. Good quality, thick paper. He unfolded what turned out to be a legal document.

A prenuptial agreement.

A sticky note on the first page included a handwritten message to Ronald. Short and sweet. It simply reminded him of the requirements for divorce. George wondered if it had come from the man's solicitor.

"I'll see you at the mead tasting." Murphy tapped his finger against the note. "Interesting. I don't remember all of the people who were at the pub. I'll ask Evan. Maybe he can give us a description. It would be intriguing to know if the solicitor did show up. Maybe that pushed Ella over the edge and made her act?"

"Or convinced her to tell her accomplice?" George thought about the napkin found at the pub. "What if the solicitor was at the brewery to serve divorce papers? What if Ronald thought she wouldn't make a scene in public?"

"One doesn't make a scene in public, does one?" Murphy returned the papers to the envelope, setting it on top of the book. "A divorce, according to the prenup, would leave her with next to nothing. She wouldn't get any of the houses. A small lump sum, but certainly not enough to keep her living as she'd become accustomed."

"That's motive. Right there in black and white."

"If you had everything, and someone could take it away from you..." Murphy gathered up the books they'd already checked and placed them back in the box. "Greed can bring out the worst in people."

"Can? Money *can* bring out the worst in people. Greed does. Money is inert. It just is." George removed the gloves from his hands. He shook his fingers out for a few seconds, hating the sensation left behind. "How do we determine if Ella was served divorce papers at the brewery that night?"

"We go back through the CCTV video from the tasting night. Maybe the cameras picked up the moment it happened?" Murphy eyed the other opened boxes. "Elwin has no idea how many of these we've opened."

"Nope."

"We could always check to see if there's anything else."

George grinned at Murphy, who was already stepping over to one of the unopened boxes. "Elwin's all bark and no bite. I'm sure it'll be fine."

FIFTEEN

MURPHY

It was, in fact, not fine.

They found nothing of interest in the rest of the boxes. When Elwin finally arrived, they were sitting outside having tea and biscuits with Seamus. He'd been the one to pick everything up from the Donelson's place.

Ella had been unpleasant as always, but nothing stood out to Seamus as suspicious. It had been a typical job, picking up rubbish from someone's place for a fee. She had insisted everything contained in the bags and boxes was rubbish.

An obvious lie. The clothes and books were definitely not rubbish. Some were worth a fair amount of money. To his mind, grief had either made her react impulsively and emotionally, or she'd hoped to avoid anyone going through his things.

Hoped in vain.

Much like Murphy had hoped Elwin would take things in stride. It had wound up being more strident than laissez-faire. He'd ripped into them for not calling immediately about the potential evidence.

"To be fair, Detective Constable Smith, we assumed the police were looking into Ella Donelson already and would've been aware of her impulsive decision to unload all of his belongings." George wasn't making eye contact, but his point struck his target nonetheless. "There were some lovely old books thrown away. Nothing says we can't peruse them for something we might want. Isn't recycling encouraged? Waste not, want not? Or some shite?"

Murphy had turned away to hide his smile. He could tell Elwin had no idea how to respond. Of course, George was technically not wrong; they'd had no reason to assume the police hadn't already combed through everything. "Well? Detective Constable?"

"Quit saying it like an insult," Elwin grumbled mulishly at him. He pinched the bridge of his nose for a moment. "You've always been a right pain in the arse, Paddy."

"Have I?"

"Can you both please remember there was a murder? Someone took a man's life." Elwin held his hand up to stop them from responding. "I know you haven't forgotten, but perhaps you haven't considered the person might still be dangerous? They might not appreciate you snooping around. I'd prefer not to be standing over your bodies, so please let us do our jobs."

"Fine." Murphy tried for sincerity. He wasn't sure Elwin believed him. "You're right. Just... make sure you're careful with the books. We found this hidden between the pages of one of them."

Elwin stared at the envelope handed over to him. He took a slow, measured breath before lifting his gaze to glower at them. "Go away now."

They decided not to poke at him any further. Seamus was definitely chuckling at them when they made a hasty retreat. It wasn't as though they hadn't found anything useful.

Checking in with Lenny, they learned he'd have both vehicles fixed by the morning. He'd gotten a mate to drive the new glass out, so it wouldn't take as long as initially feared. George drove them back to Dufftown, dropping Murphy off at the brewery on his way home.

Murphy stood outside after George had driven off, staring at the building. "Pity you can't talk to me and tell me what you saw that night. It'd make all of this so much easier."

The building didn't offer any answers. So Murphy decided to spend the afternoon going through every second of footage from the night of the tasting. There had to be something the cameras picked up.

Anything to point concretely towards the killer— or killers.

Grabbing a pint out of his fridge and a massive bag of Monster Munch Roast Beef, Murphy made himself comfortable on the sofa. He had all the windows open. It was a beautiful, breezy day; a summer storm had rolled in and cooled things off.

"Right. Time for the most boring show on the telly. My pub security camera. The Real Drinkers of Honey Bear Brewery." Murphy laughed at himself, tossing a crisp into his mouth and pressing play on the video. There were several hours of footage to go through. "This is going to take forever."

There was nothing in the first hour. Murphy caught himself drifting to sleep a few times. Then, halfway through a clip from the camera outside the brewery, he spotted something he hadn't noticed before. At one point, Ella and Darren had been outside together.

After a heated conversation, Darren had gone inside. Ella had stayed outside, pacing and seeming to mutter to herself. While she was there, another car pulled up.

Ella had seemed to recognise the driver. Murphy didn't. He was a tall bloke in a fancy suit who'd walked by her without so much as a greeting; she'd followed him into the pub.

Quickly switching to the video from inside the brewery from the same time frame, Murphy caught an exchange between the man and Ronald. A flash of white. He wondered if it was the napkin; minutes later, an envelope had been handed to Ella before the man left the pub.

Murphy watched both videos multiple times. He had no skills at lip reading, so he couldn't determine what was said—aside from Ella calling the man an arsehole. That had been easy to see. *I wonder if George wants to have dinner and watch these with me? Maybe he can figure out part of the conversation.*

Any excuse to spend time with George.

Any at all.

With their feelings out in the open, Murphy didn't have to hide anything. He could invite George over. Kiss him. Romance him. They didn't have to pretend the connection between them didn't exist.

After sending a text to invite him, Murphy decided to hop in the shower. They'd spent a fair amount of time at the recycling centre. He didn't want to feel grubby when George arrived.

First though, Murphy grabbed a screenshot of the man and sent it to Evan. He wanted to confirm if the man was a solicitor. His hunch proved right when he received a response just before he stepped into the shower.

The man on camera happened to be one of the Donelson family's preferred solicitors. Murphy was even more convinced the man had handed over the divorce papers. The one thing he couldn't figure out was why the napkin had been hidden behind the bar.

What was the point? Had someone found it and stashed it to throw away later? Or had whoever killed Ronald gotten it off the solicitor?

SIXTEEN

GEORGE

When Murphy had texted him, George had been lounging inside with Bumble. The rain had cut short his plans to be in the garden all afternoon. Instead, he grabbed a container of little savoury pastries Margo had made for him.

They were buttery and flaky, filled with a potato and mutton curry. He also had a light summer salad with veggies from her garden. It would be perfect even on a mild, rainy June afternoon.

Driving Lenny's vehicle threw him off a little. It had more sensitive brakes than his old Range Rover. He kept slamming to a stop unnecessarily hard or taking corners too sharply. His nerves were a bit ragged by the time he arrived at the brewery.

"Sorry, Bumble." George checked on him in the

back seat. He didn't seem to have enjoyed his ride in the unfamiliar vehicle. "Let's see what Murphy's got for us."

Getting out of the vehicle, George noticed the Mercedes parked directly in front of the door to the brewery. He didn't recognise it. There was nothing suspicious about it, yet his stomach started churning.

Between driving Lenny's vehicle and a surprise Mercedes, George felt his anxiety ratchet up even further. It was one of the few emotions that he found easier to identify.

The way his heart raced. The sensation of bees buzzing in his belly. He was pulled out of his thoughts by Bumble coming over to sit on his foot.

"I'm all right, Bumblebee. Just making myself freak out." George crouched down to give him a good scratch. "Better get inside before the rain starts up again."

Ringing the bell, George didn't hear anything moving inside. He tried giving Murphy a call, but he didn't answer. Odd. Bumble scratched at the door-frame, huffing with the effort to try to open the door.

George moved back to peer up at the windows of Murphy's flat. He could see lights on but no move-ment. *What's going on?*

Bumble didn't follow him. Instead, he stayed

stubbornly by the door and continued to paw at it. George returned and tried the handle; he was surprised when it twisted open.

Murphy usually didn't leave it unlocked unless he was working downstairs or Teagan was there. Neither appeared to be true. George flipped on the light by the door. The brewery workshop was empty.

No Teagan.

No Murphy.

"Paddy?" George called but received no response. "Maybe we should head upstairs?"

Bumble had no answers for him. He immediately headed for the dog bed in Murphy's office, leaving George to puzzle out the silence on his own. A noise from the pub side of the building drew both of their attention.

George walked over to the connecting door and opened it. "Murphy?"

No answer.

Stepping into the pub, George frowned at the darkness inside. Why would Murphy be moving around without a light on? He felt the wall to his left, inching along until he found the switch and flipped it.

"Who's there?"

George was caught off-guard by the voice. He

glanced around before spotting Ella Donelson behind the bar counter. "What are you doing in here? Where's Murphy?"

"Irrelevant. I want the tapes."

"Tapes?" George frowned at her in confusion. "What are you talking about?"

"The cameras." Ella pointed to the one behind the bar. "Where are the tapes?"

"Tapes? It's all digital." George shook his head. He didn't know why he was explaining anything to her. "Why are you here? How'd you get into the pub? Where's Murphy?"

"Will you shut up?"

"One's not very polite, is one?" George muttered sarcastically. He stumbled back against the wall when she came around the bar with a hunting rifle in hand. "Where. Is. Murphy?"

"I said shut up." Ella gripped the rifle tightly in her arms. She had it aimed straight at his chest. "Darren heard from a constable friend that there was a video. There was video. I have to find it. Have to get my hands on it."

While Ella kept repeating herself over and over, George managed to calm his mind down. He had to get out of "freeze" mode and into fight or flight, preferably the latter. His chances weren't brilliant when facing down an armed murderer.

George shifted closer to the door. He wondered if he could duck back into the brewery and lock her in the pub. "You killed him, didn't you? The night of the tasting. You dumped dry ice into his drink and gave it to him."

"He made a mockery of me." Ella sneered angrily. She treated the rifle with a casualness that only served to increase his worry. "I took a class on creating mixed drinks that included a warning about the dangers of dry ice in cocktails."

"Did you?" George kept a close eye on the movements of the rifle in her hand. He had no idea if she knew how to use the thing, but he wasn't taking any chances. An angry fool with a gun was still dangerous even if they weren't sharpshooters. "Ronald did seem to be an unpleasant bloke."

"He was. One expects some level of refinement from a family such as his." Ella lowered the barrel of the rifle slightly. "He had affairs yet had the temerity to file for divorce after I dared to have one of my own."

"So you put dry ice in his drink?"

"He never knew. Such a glutton. Tossed back the

142

drink without even looking at it." Ella seemed completely disgusted by her deceased husband.

Listening to her rant about her husband and her plot, George inched closer to the door. Just a little bit more, and he'd be able to bolt out of the door. He had no idea where Murphy was, but he had to get out of the room and call the police.

For a split second, Ella spun around toward the camera. She aimed the rifle at it, wavering on her heels. George wondered if she'd been drinking before he took advantage of her distraction to dash out the open door.

He slammed it behind him and then locked it. "Shite. Shite. Shite. Where's my phone?"

Breathing through the adrenaline-pumped panic, George scrambled away in case she decided to shoot through it. He raced over to lock the front door as well. It wouldn't do for her to find another way at him.

Phone.

Where's my phone?

"Oh for...." George groaned when he realised the phone was in his hand. He immediately dialled the police, trying to keep his voice clear despite the shakiness. The dispatcher promised they were on their way. They tried to keep him on the line, but all he wanted was to find Murphy. "We have to be quiet, Bumble."

Lifting Bumble into his arms, George crept up the stairs. He pushed the door open and couldn't swallow back a shout when a shadowy figure loomed in front of him. It took a second for him to realise it was Murphy in nothing but a towel, with his hair and beard dripping with water.

"I heard sounds while I was in the shower."

George didn't hear a word Murphy had said. He couldn't tear his gaze away from the bare chest in front of him. The muscles, the slight softness, the bristly hair still damp from the shower. It was a lot to take in, and he wanted to enjoy the moment; then he remembered the murderer downstairs. "Ella. Rifle. Oh my god. You have a tattoo. Never mind. I called the police."

Murphy reached out to take George by the arms. "I need you to take a few deep breaths for me, alright? Take a second. It's going to be okay."

"Ella was in the pub. She had a rifle." George breathed in deeply and tried not to focus too much on the intricate Celtic design on Murphy's chest. "She... wanted the security footage because she thought it caught her putting dry ice in Ronald's glass."

"Well, shite."

"She had a rifle." George reiterated the most important part in his mind.

"You called the police?"

George had managed to get his breathing under control. He set Bumble down when he wiggled in his arms. "I did. Oh my god."

"Why don't you have a seat? Not much we can do until they arrive. I'm not anxious to confront an armed killer." Murphy led him over to the sofa. Bumble had already gone over and flopped down on his bed. "You okay?"

"Why don't you go put some bloody clothes on?" George was finding himself highly distracted by the almost naked Murphy. He grimaced at his own turn of phrase. "Poor choice of wording."

"Having problems?" Murphy teased. "Fine, fine. Let me finish drying off. You might watch the window for the police."

Once Murphy had gone to get dressed, George crept over to the window. He immediately noticed the Mercedes was gone. Ella had clearly come to her senses and made a run for it.

A few moments later, several police vehicles raced up the lane towards the brewery. George left Bumble in his bed and went downstairs to meet them. Murphy came bounding down the stairs behind him a few moments later, still dragging a T-shirt over his head.

"We should meet them outside." Murphy stepped up behind him. He rested his arm across George's shoulders while holding his laptop in his other hand. "I've got the CCTV hooked up to this computer, so we can hopefully watch what she did."

The encounter with Ella had shaken George up a fair bit. He'd never come face-to-barrel with a gun ever in his life. The most dangerous things in his life were bee stings and an overenthusiastic pug.

"You all right, Buzz?" Murphy paused at the door. "They can wait."

"Fine." George had meant to sound firm, but his voice came out shaky. "Honestly. I'm okay. I wasn't hurt."

Murphy squeezed his arm around George's shoulders, further drawing him into his side. "Nothing wrong with admitting that you went through something terrifying."

"I froze at first. You always hear people talking about fight or flight. But it was like I hit pause on my brain." George reached out to open the door since Murphy's hands were both occupied. "We don't want the police to think we're being held hostage."

SEVENTEEN

MURPHY

Despite having opened the door, George made no move to step through it. Murphy had a feeling he was completely overwhelmed by everything. It wasn't about to get any easier; it was likely to get noisier.

"Where're your fancy headphones?" Murphy knew he kept noise-cancelling earbuds on him. "Why not pop those in? They might help dull the roar that will be the police."

"I..." George shook his head.

It was like watching a turtle pull back into his shell. George was clearly retreating into himself. Murphy decided the best thing to do was find him a quiet space to himself.

"Right. Okay. Here's what we're going to do. I'm

going to lead you into my office. It's nice, warm, and quiet in there. I've even got a blanket over the back of my chair. We'll find your earbuds and put those in." Murphy kept his voice low and steady. He kept his arm gently around George's shoulders, using the hold to guide him across the brewery. "There. Comfiest chair in the whole building. Let's see if we can find your headphones."

The earbuds wound up being in his pocket. Murphy helped him get those in his ears and wrapped the blanket around him. He left the lights dimmed, trying to minimise any sensory issues for him.

With that settled, Murphy went outside to deal with the police. He hoped with a video of what happened. Then they'd be able to wait on questioning George.

"There you are. What the hell is going on?" Sarah was pacing outside of the brewery. "We got a call about a gun."

"Here. I've got a video." Murphy set the laptop on the bonnet of her car. He pressed Play, letting all of them watch. "This is from before she broke into the pub."

While they watched, someone turned a light on and then off again in the pub. A figure slowly walked inside and began peering up at the ceiling. She eventually stood directly in front of one of the cameras, tilting her face straight into the lens.

"Ella Donelson," Sarah muttered.

The angle also gave them a clear view of the rifle in her arms. Ella was almost manic in how she paced around the pub, peering behind the bar counter. It was apparent she was hunting for something.

Then after almost ten minutes, Ella froze in place. She slowly stood up. Her attention shifted across the room to the door that led into the brewery.

Pulling up a second video frame, they were able to watch from two different perspectives. They watched the confrontation. Murphy grew angrier with each passing second of the rifle aimed at George.

Murphy wanted to reach through the laptop screen and yank the weapon out of Ella's hands. "I'll sodding—"

"You are surrounded by the police. Do *not* finish that sentence." Sarah placed a calming hand on his shoulder. "Your beekeeper is fine. Probably shaken but alive and uninjured. So do not say the words you were just thinking."

His cousin made an excellent point, so he snapped his mouth shut. He glowered at the laptop screen instead. It was no wonder George had been completely overwrought by the situation.

"I'm going to have to ask him some questions." Sarah finally commented after they'd viewed the video multiple times. She'd sent several constables and Elwin out to try to locate Ella Donelson. "I need his witness statement on the record."

"Can you wait? He..." Murphy trailed off. He didn't want to go into too many personal details. George could share what he wanted to about it. "He was overwhelmed and needed some time to calm down."

"Okay." Sarah flipped her notebook shut. She leaned against the side of her vehicle. "She's danger-ous. I can't say for certain she killed her husband without speaking to George and to her, but she didn't break into the pub while armed for no reason at all. So I'm going to ask you both to be careful. Maybe come stay at my place or something? I don't want you to be alone."

"I'll figure something out. Not leaving George to fend for himself, since she's seen him. And everyone and their mother knows where our Buzz lives." Murphy closed his laptop after sending Sarah the footage from the video. He scratched absently at his beard. "I can't understand what she'd expected to do here? She had to think we'd already given you the video the day of the murder."

"If she did kill her husband, I doubt she's thinking very clearly at this point. In my experience, the closer to getting caught someone is, the more irrationally they behave." Sarah held a hand up when her phone rang. She wandered off to have a brief conversation. Murphy couldn't make out any of it, so he waited for her to return after a few minutes. "They found her Mercedes at the Donelson estate. No sign of her anywhere. The family has several other vehicles. At least two are unaccounted for, and she's likely switched to one of them."

"She could've made a run for it."

"Possibly. I'd still like you and Murphy to be cautious until she's been caught. We don't know the whole story yet. We have no idea who all might be involved." She stowed her notebook away and her phone. "Listen, I'm leaving one of the constables here for the next few hours in case she comes back. Where are you going?"

"Pack a few things and go to George's cottage. I can sleep on his couch. We'll even have a guard dog." Murphy grinned when Sarah huffed in disbelief. "Bumble's more than capable of giving a warning alert if anyone breaks into the cottage."

"And what? Snore them to death?" Sarah shook her head at him. "Just be careful, all right? You're my least annoying cousin."

"High praise." Murphy took his laptop and stepped back towards the pub. He waved to the constable, who was sitting in a parked car. "Fancy a cuppa?"

"Nah. Better not." He waved him off.

Once Sarah had driven away, Murphy returned to the brewery. He set his laptop on one of the tables and went to check on George, who had managed to curl up in Murphy's office chair. His eyes were closed, and his head bopped a little to whatever music played on his earbuds.

Murphy watched him for a moment. He didn't want to startle him after what he'd experienced earlier. "George?"

There was no response initially. Murphy waited him out, since he'd seen George tense ever so slightly. Finally, after several minutes, he reached up to remove the earbuds.

"Sarah ready for me?" George's voice was quiet and slightly shaky.

"I talked her into waiting. She's focusing on finding Ella. I gave her all the camera footage, so your statement can wait." Murphy leaned against the doorframe. He wanted to give George as much space as possible. "She did suggest we avoid being alone, and I stay somewhere other than the brewery until Ella's captured."

"Margo's got a spare room and a comfortable couch. So three people and two yappy dogs are better than one?" George still had the blanket wrapped tightly around him. "I'll text her to see if she minds."

"You okay? Anything I can do to help?"

George shrugged. He tugged at the blanket, adjusting it around his shoulders. "I wouldn't say no to a hug."

"You sure?" Murphy moved further into his office. He crouched in front of where George sat in his desk chair. "I don't want to make things worse."

"You couldn't." George let the blanket fall away from him. He still had his earbuds clutched in his hand when he threw his arms around Murphy. "Thought she'd killed you."

"What?"

"When I got here, all I saw was Ella Donelson with a rifle in your pub. No sign of you. I didn't hear anything. There was nothing at all to indicate where you were." George reached out to grasp Murphy's shirt. He clutched at it tightly, dragging him forward a little. "Next time you throw a mead tasting? Maybe leave the dry ice out of the party supplies list."

"Not a bad idea."

George laughed a little hysterically. He eased his hold on Murphy's shirt and sat back in the chair. His cheeks were flushed as though embarrassed at what had happened. "Brings a whole new meaning to bubble, bubble, toil and trouble."

"Let's see if we can avoid the wicked part that comes next."

EIGHTEEN

GEORGE

NEITHER OF THEM WAS SURPRISED WHEN MARGO readily agreed to have them over. She didn't enjoy going out, but having company was right up her alley. So George sat with Bumble in Murphy's living room, waiting while he gathered up a change of clothes for himself.

"Why don't we stop in the village on the way to Margo's? We can pick up snacks or a takeaway. Something to make up for crashing her quiet evening at home." Murphy had a green duffle bag that looked old enough to be from his military days. He also had his laptop under one arm. "Going to keep an eye on the cameras in case she shows back up—also make sure I lock the doors."

"When we get there, I want to look at the video

from the night our vehicles were vandalised." George kept thinking about the figure he'd seen running away.

"You're wondering if it was Ella?"

"Or Darren, on her behalf. Both are clearly talking to one another. He told her there was a video." George wondered if they'd both been involved in the murder. Or perhaps Darren had figured out Ella did it and was now trying to protect his lover. "I can't help thinking there's something we've missed on the video."

"We'll watch all of the videos I have from the tasting and from the night the windows were broken. We may spot the needle in the haystack, between the three of us." Murphy led the way out of the apartment. He made sure to lock all of the doors. "Here's hoping she doesn't try to break in for a second time."

"No one's that daft."

"Desperation makes people do dangerous and daft things." Murphy took the keys to the vehicle. George had no interest in driving it again. His nerves had only just begun to calm down. "Ella definitely has to know the police have zeroed in on her as their suspect."

"She did confess to me that she'd done it." George hadn't been entirely coherent when he'd spoken to Murphy the first time. The cameras in the pub had no audio on them. "I wish I'd put my phone on to record it. She can always say I'm lying, and I've no proof."

"Aside from the rifle pointed at your chest?" Murphy opened the car doors. He put his bag in the boot while George got Bumble secured in the back seat. "Still want to swing by the village and then your cottage before heading to Margo's?"

"We can skip the village. I've got plenty of snacks. But Ella pointing a gun at me doesn't prove she murdered her husband." George believed her confession. It had been too raw to be a lie. She'd barely been aware of his presence, ranting about all of the reasons why Ronald had deserved to die. "Not sure the police can arrest her based on my saying she admitted it."

"Probably not, but it may help them in their investigation." Murphy pulled his phone out of his pocket. He began typing out a text. "I'm telling Sarah what you heard from Ella. If nothing else, she'll want your statement."

"Right." He pulled on his seat belt. His fingers had finally stopped shaking like a leaf. "Not sure what frightened me more. The gun in front of me—or the knowledge she'd probably already killed you."

"Just glad nothing happened to either of us."

"Aside from having the life scared out of me."

"Aside from that." Murphy took his hand; his thumb rubbed over George's knuckles. The touch was comforting. It soothed some of the rawness he still felt. "Right. Change of subject, because obsessing over Ella Donelson isn't going to help either of our nerves. I'd really hoped to take you on a proper date."

"What does proper even mean when it comes to dating or feelings? Sounds very much like when people say a 'real' relationship or use 'normal.' I've never been good at either of those things." George stared out the window. He'd often analysed how his friends and family talked about their romances. "Is it weird how I feel like we're deep in a relationship already because I've known you for so long and always felt so connected to you?"

"Not weird. Not at all." Murphy squeezed his hand. "But I still want to go on a proper date."

"After the wicked widow is dealt with." George had never been overly tactile in any of his previous relationships. He could be finicky about it, but Murphy seemed to know when to ease back. It helped him relax even further. "Let's just hope the police catch up to her quickly."

"They'll do their best."

It didn't exactly strike confidence in George. He wondered if maybe they should stay somewhere closer to the village. Maybe at a cottage not closely connected to either of them.

Everyone knew Margo.

They all knew she was his cousin.

"What if Darren discovered Ella had killed Ronald? He might decide to protect her instead of turning her in." George thought their vandal was the former, not the latter. Something in the person's gait when they'd fled the scene didn't strike him as Ella Donelson. "We're missing part of the story."

"Let's just hope it doesn't wind up being the end of our story."

"Happy thoughts, Paddy." George rested his head back against the seat. He felt drained from the events of the day. "Happy thoughts."

NINETEEN

MURPHY

THE EVENING HAD BEEN SUBDUED. DESPITE THE snacks they'd picked up from his cottage, George hadn't been hungry. He'd made his excuses and disappeared into Margo's spare room.

"He's going to watch one of his shows. It'll help him after shutting down the way he did." Margo cleared up the food. She carried things into the kitchen. "You're good for him."

"Oh?"

"Not many people are patient with him. They don't have a good grasp of knowing when to give him the space he needs." Margo went over to let Bumble and Treacle out into the garden. "I'll let these two of run some of the energy off. They'll probably sleep together in the bed by the hearth."

"All right."

"I imagine they'll wake you up at least once. Poor Bumble's an elderly wee bloke. He might need a walk." Margo leaned against the door, watching the dogs race the length of her garden. "Murphy."

He sat up quickly at the sharp, hushed tone in her voice. "What is it?"

"Someone's out there." Margo whistled for the dogs. She repeated it a few times. "It's dark enough I can't quite see, but a shadow moved down by the cluster of trees at the end of the garden. They must've walked up the lane, then come through the hedge."

"You sure it wasn't one of the dogs?"

"Not unless they suddenly began walking on two feet." Margo gave yet another whistle. Bumble finally trundled into the cottage. "Treacle?"

Murphy had got to his feet. He placed a hand on her shoulder, pulling away from the door. "Call Sarah."

"Treacle's still out there." Margo tried whistling for him again, stopping when Murphy placed a hand on her arm. "What?"

"Let's not draw too much attention to the cottage." Murphy grabbed the nearby iron fire poker.

It had an intricately designed elephant on the top. "Call Sarah. If you can't get her, call 999."

"Don't break that. I had it custom-made."

"What the hell am I going to do with this?" Murphy muttered to himself. He was taking a piece of wrought iron into a gunfight and didn't like his odds. *Unto the breach.*

Moving away from the cottage lights, Murphy tried to disappear into the shadows along the edge of the garden. He could hear Ella Donelson's voice. She seemed to be arguing with herself about what to do.

The slight slur in her voice made him wonder if she was drunk. He finally caught sight of her, struggling to unhook her clothing from the hedge. She'd trapped herself while shoving through into the garden.

It would've been comical if he hadn't spotted the rifle in her arms. There was nothing funny about a deadly weapon in the hands of a drunk. She'd be even more unpredictable.

Murphy edged his way behind the trees, trying to get closer to her. He whispered for Treacle, but the dog was nowhere to be seen. *Sodding Chihuahua. Where've you run off to?*

Coming out of the shadows to her left, Murphy remained out of sight. Ella continued to try to yank herself free from the hedge. He thought she was trying to avoid ripping her shirt. It probably cost more than his car. Ella had always cared about showing her wealth and status in every way possible. Her clothes had to be designer—even if they were bordering on hideous to his unsophisticated eye.

She was wearing a fancy silk-looking blouse with a skirt and high heels. He had no idea how she'd even made it up the lane in them. Not practical for a walk anywhere but especially on the rocky, uneven path behind the cottage.

Murphy froze when a branch snapped under his boot. *Shite*.

Ella glanced around wildly before spotting him. "You."

"Did tiptoeing through the garden go wrong for you?" Murphy knew it would be several minutes before any of the police arrived. They were all out searching for Ella—and she'd decided to show up at Margo's cottage. "Need a hand getting free?"

"You. You. This is all your fault." Ella jabbed the rifle in his direction. "Your tasting. Such a dismal, grungy pub. I should've done it another way. But the dry ice was there. I thought the police would assume your daft little server made a mistake."

"You didn't count on the cameras."

"Who has CCTV cameras inside their establishment?" Ella gave one last pull, and her blouse ripped, freeing her from the grasp of the hedge. "I had to do it. He was going to file for divorce."

"One couldn't have that, could one?" Murphy was intrigued by her dropping the affectation. "Why not fight the prenup? Surely you wouldn't be left with nothing."

"I deserved all of it."

Right.

"Of course." Murphy shifted a little closer to her. He hoped he'd be able to lunge for her rifle before she fired a shot at him. "Of course."

Ella stumbled a little. She seemed more tipsy than sloshed. "Darren promised to fix everything for me. Weak fool. He couldn't even take care of his wife."

"Take care of her?"

"She asked too many questions about Ronnie's death and claimed she'd seen me by the drinks. She saw me bring the glass to him. He was too much of a coward to shut her up." Ella had a loose grip on the rifle. It made him nervous. "I'll have to deal with her after I'm finished here."

"Finished how?" Murphy was desperate to keep her talking, anything to give the police time to arrive and intervene. He held the fire poker down by his side. She hadn't noticed it yet. "Why not make a run for it? Don't you have a private plane? Jet off to some island somewhere. Isn't that what people like you do?"

With a hiss of anger at him, Ella raised the rifle towards him. Murphy had no time to do anything with the poker aside from maybe fling it in her direction. He adjusted the iron in his hand, considering his options.

Before either of them could react, Treacle darted out from underneath the hedge. He latched onto Ella's ankle. She shrieked like a banshee and dropped the rifle, attempting to kick the nimble Chihuahua darting around her feet.

Using the distraction to his advantage, Murphy rushed forward to grab the rifle. He tossed it out of reach behind him and caught Ella by the wrists, managing to stop her flailing. She kicked him hard in the shins, but he held fast, not wanting her to escape.

"Paddy!"

"Down at the end of the garden," Murphy called back to his cousin. He was hesitant to move, since he had such a tight hold on Ella. "Quit your wiggling. I'm not letting you go."

The police caught up to them seconds later and

took Ella along with her rifle into custody. Murphy was left standing in the garden with his cousin. Sarah didn't seem amused by him.

"So, I found your suspect for you." Murphy still had the fire poker in his hand. He held it to the side when Sarah yanked him into a hug. "I'm good. Not a scratch on me."

They heard Ella shouting at the constables who were leading her away. She blamed everyone but her own actions, including Treacle. Murphy tried not to laugh at the ridiculousness of how things had ended.

"She literally would've gotten away with it except for our meddling and the dog." Murphy grinned at Sarah, who groaned and smacked him on the arm. "Too soon?"

"Go snog your new boyfriend and leave the professionals to their work." Sarah caught the back of his shirt. "Try to keep yourselves out of my cases from now on? Please."

"Going on the top of my to-do list. Avoid any further entanglements with murder inquiries to preserve all of our sanities. Also, kissing." Murphy walked away before she could scold him further. George was waiting for him when he returned to the relative calm of the cottage. "I've strict orders from the esteemed Detective Constable Baird."

"Oh?" George sat on the edge of the couch. "What orders?"

"I'm under advisement to snog my boyfriend and avoid dead bodies." Murphy managed a tired smile when George stood and took a step towards him. "What do you think?"

"Solid advice. More kissing, less murder. I wholeheartedly agree."

BE on the lookout for book two, HONEY BEE MURDER. Looking for more MM cosy mysteries from Dahlia? Check out two fun series: **THE GRASMERE COTTAGE MYSTERY TRILOGY** and **LONDON PODCAST MYSTERY SERIES.**

ACKNOWLEDGMENTS

A massive thank-you to my brilliant betas who take my first draft and help me turn it into something legible. To Becky, Olivia, and all the fantastic people at Tangled Tree and Hot Tree Publishing. And also to my beloved hubby, who keeps me from losing my mind while I'm stressing over word counts.

And, lastly, thank you, readers, for following me on my writing journey. I hope you enjoyed *Honey Mead Murder* and are looking forward to book two.

ABOUT THE AUTHOR

Thanks for reading Honey Mead Murder. I do hope you enjoyed my story. I appreciate your help in spreading the word, including telling a friend. Before you go, it would mean so much to me if you would take a few minutes to write a review and share how you feel about my story so others may find my work. Reviews really do help readers find books. Please leave a review on your favorite book site.

Don't miss out on New Releases, Exclusive Giveaways, and much more!

Join my newsletter:

http://eepurl.com/QonoX

Join my reader group:

www.facebook.com/groups/ 1108750876162947

I'd love to hear from you directly, too. Please feel free to email me at dahlia@dahliadonovan.com or check out my website https://dahliadonovan. com/ for updates.

Dahlia Donovan wrote her first romance series after a crazy dream about shifters and damsels in distress. She prefers irreverent humour and unconventional characters. An autistic and occasional hermit, her life wouldn't be complete without her husband and her massive collection of books and video games.

facebook.com/dahliadonovan

twitter.com/DahliaDonovan

instagram.com/dahliadonovanauthor

pinterest.com/dahliadonovan

ABOUT THE PUBLISHER

Tangled Tree Publishing loves all things tangled and aims to bring darker, twisted, and more mind-boggling books to its readers. Publishing adult and new adult fiction, TTPubs are all about diverse reads in mystery, suspense, thrillers, and crime.

For more details, head to www.TANGLEDTREEPUBLISHING.COM

 facebook.com/tangledtreepublishing

twitter.com/ttpubs

 tiktok.com/@hottreepublishing